Michael Underwood and The Murder Room

>>> This title is part of The Murder Room, our series dedicated to making available out-of-print or hard-to-find titles by classic crime writers.

Crime fiction has always held up a mirror to society. The Victorians were fascinated by sensational murder and the emerging science of detection; now we are obsessed with the forensic detail of violent death. And no other genre has so captivated and enthralled readers.

Vast troves of classic crime writing have for a long time been unavailable to all but the most dedicated frequenters of second-hand bookshops. The advent of digital publishing means that we are now able to bring you the backlists of a huge range of titles by classic and contemporary crime writers, some of which have been out of print for decades.

From the genteel amateur private eyes of the Golden Age and the femmes fatales of pulp fiction, to the morally ambiguous hard-boiled detectives of mid twentieth-century America and their descendants who walk our twenty-first century streets, The Murder Room has it all. **>>>**

The Murder Room
Where Criminal Minds Meet

themurderroom.com

T0352013

Michael Underwood (1916–1992)

Michael Underwood (the pseudonym of John Michael Evelyn) was born in Worthing, Sussex and educated at Christ Church College, Oxford. He was called to the Bar in 1939 and served in the British army during World War Two. He returned to work in the Department of Public Prosecutions until his retirement in 1976, and wrote almost 50 crime novels informed by his career in the law. His five series characters include Sergeant Nick Atwell and lawyer Rosa Epton, of whom is was said by the *Washington Post* that she 'outdoes Perry Mason'.

By Michael Underwood

Standalone titles

A Crime Apart
Shem's Demise
The Silent Liars
Anything But the Truth

Smooth Justice
Victim of Circumstance
A Clear Case of Suicide
The Hand of Fate

A Trout in the Milk

Michael Underwood

An Orion book

Copyright © Isobel Mackenzie 1971

The right of Michael Underwood to be identified as the author of this
work has been asserted in accordance with the Copyright, Designs and
Patents Act 1988.

This edition published by
The Orion Publishing Group Ltd
Orion House
5 Upper St Martin's Lane
London WC2H 9EA

An Hachette UK company
A CIP catalogue record for this book is available from the British Library

ISBN 978 1 4719 0792 0

www.orionbooks.co.uk

Some circumstantial evidence is
very strong, as when you find a
trout in the milk.

Thoreau

An urgent tearing sound halted Robin Appleman in his tracks.

'Damn and blast!' He looked down with dismay at the sleeve of his barrister's gown which a moment before had been proudly billowing, but which now hung like the broken wing of a blackbird. 'Oh blast!' he repeated as his eye caught sight of the loose, jutting hinge of one of the robing-room lockers.

A stranger might have thought his language remarkably restrained in the circumstances and have attributed this to the Old Bailey's grave, repressive aura. But in fact it was Robin's own strict Nonconformist upbringing which continued to inhibit him, so that the two expletives he used were the worst in his vocabulary. Furthermore, he was someone who frequently suffered uneasy forebodings of hellfire, even after three years of living in London away from home while he had been working for his Bar exams.

But now he was a full-blown barrister of four months' standing ... A barrister with a shredded sleeve to his gown ... And worse, a barrister who was already late for Court.

It was only a few days ago that James Geddy, his pupil-master, had gently but firmly reproved him for too often arriving at Court at the last minute – or just after it.

'Clients don't like their Counsel looking as though he'd just run all the way from Fulham, dressing on the way.'

Robin had nodded in vigorous assent. 'I know. I'm terribly sorry, it's just that ...'

'It's just that you're one of nature's unpunctual animals, Robin. But you must overcome this ... not sloth, heaven knows nobody could accuse you of being slothful or unalert once you're there ... this penchant for the last-minute arrival. As an advocate, you're in the front row of the chorus and you can't get away with it.' He had smiled in a way to remove any sting from his rebuke. 'At the moment, as a pupil, you're only in the second row, but that still doesn't mean you can sneak in unnoticed.'

And that had only been the day before the Manion trial had begun. For the past three days he had been sitting behind his pupil-master in Number 1 Court where Geddy was defending a man about whom the public at large had long since formed its conclusions, namely that he was one of the more dangerous members of society who belonged behind bars for as long as anyone liked to suggest. For Frank Manion was without doubt one of the top league criminals who normally managed to keep themselves several moves beyond the reach of the police. But now he was fighting desperately for his freedom.

Tucking his notebook beneath his arm and bunching the torn sleeve into his other hand, Robin streaked off towards Court. There was still a chance, he thought, that he'd make it before the judge. It was usually a couple of minutes after the half hour before those imperious knocks heralded Mr Justice Tyler's entry. And, according to Robin's watch, it was only twenty-nine minutes past.

The concourse outside the main Courts was thronged with people as he thrust his way towards Number 1 Court. Once he found himself forcing a passage through a group of waiting jurors.

'That young man's in a bloody hurry,' one of them observed sourly, as Robin cannoned off him.

'They're all in a bloody hurry *outside* Court,' his neighbour replied. 'But get 'em inside and they seem to think you want to spend your lifetime there as well. Takes 'em ten minutes to put the right question and then they have to go through it all over again.'

'That's to make sure we've got the point. They don't know what's going on in our minds as we sit there listening.'

'Wouldn't mind their knowing what's going on in mine! Wouldn't want some of the ones I've heard these past few days defending me, I can tell you.'

'A citizen's highest public duty, the judge called it yesterday.'

'And his biggest waste of bloody time! Anyway, let's hope our next case has a bit of spice.'

By this time, Robin had reached Court. As he shot through the outer swing doors, his heart sank for he saw the judge already in his place. He was about to push stealthily through the inner glass-panelled doors when his way was suddenly barred. It was the tall, thin police officer with the humorous face who was holding the door against his entry, at the same time mouthing at him through the glass. He looked like some comical fish in an aquarium tank and Robin replied with his own more urgent signs of wishing to enter. But all the officer did was to put his finger to his lips, roll his eyes dramatically and turn his back.

Glancing past him, Robin saw that a witness was in the box taking the oath. This explained everything since Mr Justice Tyler could be guaranteed to instigate an immediate reign of terror in Court if anyone so much as scratched an ear when the oath was being taken. He would command silence as though for the last roll-call and then deliver a stern homily on the solemnity attaching to the swearing of a witness or a juror. Thereafter, the desire to cough, squirm or scratch became, for many, almost unendurable. But it was generally recognised that every judge must be allowed one idiosyncrasy, and this was Tyler, J's.

The tall back removed itself and the door was held open just enough to let him slide past.

'Ssh!' the officer hissed with another exaggerated gesture of compelling silence. He plucked at Robin's gown as he went to pass. 'Your wig's on crooked, Mr Appleman.'

'Oh, thanks.' Robin's hand flew up to straighten his barristerial plumage, which still caused him moments of embarrassment when he happened to catch sight of himself.

He slipped into his seat behind James Geddy, opened his notebook and began writing. All in one continuing movement.

Geddy turned his head and Robin leaned forward.

'I'm terribly sorry, I had a bit of an accident ...' His voice trailed away apologetically as he met Geddy's coolly quizzical gaze and he bent with increased fervour over his notebook.

The witness in the box was Detective Chief Superintendent Peters who was the officer in charge of the case. The prosecution's evidence was drawing to a close and would be followed by James Geddy's submission of no case to answer on at least some of the counts in the indictment. Then, unless the judge threw the whole case out, would come the make or break of every criminal trial, the accused's own performance in the witness box.

In a matter of seconds, Robin had forgotten all his discomfiture as he became wholly absorbed in his note-taking role. For years he had dreamed of becoming a barrister and now here he was playing a part, important if mute, in one of the most talked-about trials of the year. Important because, although only a pupil without any standing in the case, he knew that Geddy relied on him to do more than take a good note, to pick up what he himself might miss.

When the luncheon adjournment came, Peters was still giving evidence, but was unlikely to be in the box for much longer. James Geddy, who had been cross-examining him for half an hour, was giving a demonstration of how a skilled advocate tackles a tough, no-quarter-giving adversary who was additionally an extremely experienced witness. It was an exercise in not attempting the impossible, but of extracting the one or two points which could not be denied the defence. Senior police officers didn't suddenly crack up in the witness-box, nor was Peters one of those given to overstating his evidence. He was quiet, temperate, unshakeable – and deadly.

At one o'clock, Mr Justice Tyler who had scarcely intervened throughout the morning's proceedings announced that the Court would adjourn until five minutes past two.

James Geddy turned round to Robin. 'Not much change to be got from a witness like Peters. It's like throwing pebbles at the Rock of Gibraltar.'

Robin, who had been admiring his pupil-master's handling of this implacable witness, nodded. 'I don't see what more you could have achieved.'

'I know, but one always hopes for miracles even though one doesn't count on them. I'd like to look through your note of my cross-examination, but that can wait till after lunch. Coming to the mess?'

'James, just before you go . . .'

Geddy turned to find Peter Strange, the senior of the two Treasury Counsel prosecuting in the case, approaching him.

'Don't tell me anything you shouldn't, but I take it you're going to submit on Count One? Frankly, I don't see that I have any answer . . .'

'Or any evidence,' Geddy broke in, with a smile.

Strange shrugged, then lowering his voice said, 'We both know the form in this sort of case. It's all a question of where the witnesses think their better interests lie. I've not only had one ratting on me in the box but another failing to appear at all.' His voice had an angry edge at the now empty dock and at the innocent back of Adrian Slatter, Geddy's instructing solicitor, who was gathering up his strewn papers at a table in the well of the Court where he sat immediately in front of his counsel.

James Geddy made no comment. He would have felt the same had he been prosecuting. 'To answer your question, Peter, I certainly shall be submitting and it won't be confined to Count One.'

'I see. Well, thanks for telling me. You can't possibly hope to get out of the lot at this juncture.'

It was Geddy's turn to shrug. 'Difficult to know with old Tyler. He rarely gives one any sort of indication of what's going on in his mind, except when he thinks he hears a pin drop during the oath.'

Peter Strange laughed. 'I hear he's likely to go up to the Court of Appeal soon.'

'Put three of him in a row and you really will have a

picture of inscrutable justice.' He turned back to Robin who was talking to the solicitor.

'Anything you want done during the adjournment, Mr Geddy?' Slatter asked.

'No, thanks. Manion realises he may be in the box before the end of the day?'

'Yes, though he's hoping your submission will save him the necessity. But you'll find him a good witness.'

'I hope the jury do as well! I must say, I can't recall a client who ever showed such a lively interest in his trial. He's the most prolific note scribbler I've come across.'

Slatter seemed to colour slightly as though this was a reproach on him. 'I only pass on the ones which seem relevant,' he said defensively.

'My dear chap, I'm not accusing you of anything, though on the whole it's not a habit to be encouraged among one's clients. I don't believe I can recall a single occasion when a client has either reminded me of something I'd forgotten or told me something I needed to know.' He gave a small laugh. 'But I'd probably be as active if I were sitting in the dock listening to someone trying to defend me.'

'And Manion isn't the easiest of clients from a solicitor's point of view,' Slatter said, again in a slightly defensive tone.

'I'm quite sure he's not! Well, see you after the adjournment.'

Later when they were having lunch in the Bar mess, Robin said, 'I get the impression that Adrian Slatter doesn't care for his client very much.'

'Can't say that I blame him,' Geddy said, trying to spear an elusive piece of potato on his plate. He paused a second with the potato on the end of his fork and then slowly put it in his mouth. Robin had a feeling that he had been on the verge of making a similar comment about Slatter himself, but had balked at an indiscretion which might be overheard.

Robin had heard a good deal about Adrian Slatter before he ever met him. He sent a lot of work to 4 Mulberry Court and obviously had a high opinion of James Geddy whom he often instructed in his more important cases. Those in Chambers were, in general, fairly divided in their view of him as a person, though everyone agreed that he was competent, that his briefs were well prepared and, most strongly in his favour, that he paid up promptly, which was more than could be said for a good many solicitors in criminal practice. This last was, in the eyes of some, his most attractive feature.

Robin, however, had also rather taken to him as a person. It may have had something to do with the fact they were both self-made in the sense that each came from a family which had not previously claimed any professional men in its ranks. This formed an unconscious bond in a profession which is still largely manned by so-called public school types. There was also a slightly anxious air about him which evoked Robin's sympathy. And, lastly, there had been the completely different physical image of the man from what he had been expecting. This is always something of a shock. You build up a picture of someone and then you meet him and he doesn't remotely resemble the person you had imagined.

He had never expected that a solicitor, who had, as clients, some of the biggest criminals in town and whose managing clerk looked just like one of them, would turn out to have the guise of the man he had met for the first time a week before the trial opened. Anxious and rather lonely looking, Adrian Slatter had also appeared much younger than Robin had expected. Robin decided that he was probably unfairly judged by Chambers. Certainly Donald, the clerk, liked him, and not only on account of the work he sent to Chambers or the promptness with which his cheques arrived afterwards. And Donald was a sound judge of men, as well as being an extremely good clerk. It was he who had told Robin of Slatter's reputation as a lady's man when Robin had said that he looked a lonely sort of person.

James Geddy's voice suddenly broke in on his thoughts.
'Finished, Robin?'

'Yes.'

'Sure? You look as though you might be hoping for another helping of that syrup pudding.'

'No, I've finished, though it was jolly good.'

'Well, let's find a quiet corner. I'd like to run through some of the points of my submission with you.'

The case against Frank Manion, never as strong as the prosecution had hoped, had been seriously eroded by the defection of two crown witnesses. It would probably be argued later that the police would have done better to have waited until they could have mounted a stronger case, but this would be ignoring the realities, as well as smacking of hindsight.

Among the realities was a man named Ricky Pitts who had been found one night in a state of collapse in a gutter and who, in a probably unconsidered moment, alleged that he had been beaten up by Manion in his office at Frank's Tavern, a night-club and the West End headquarters of Manion's various enterprises.

This had led to Manion's arrest and his immediate denial that anything of the sort had happened. He could only suggest that Ricky Pitts, never one of Society's more stable members, had better have the inside of his head examined, not just the outside bandaged, if he was going to throw accusations of that sort around.

As the police now had him under lock and key, they not unreasonably decided to see whether they couldn't find a bit more to pin on him. The very fact that he was in custody might encourage some of those who had suffered in their dealings with him to come forward with evidence.

And so it proved, though the result was something closer to a trickle than a floodtide of accusations.

At all events it led to Manion facing trial at the Old Bailey on four counts. The first alleged an offence of causing grievous bodily harm with intent and related to the assault on Ricky Pitts. The next two were allegations of blackmail and referred to the extortion of £1500 in one instance and just over £2000 in the other from someone named Sam Lusk. The fourth related to an offence of attempting to obtain money by deception and hinged entirely on the inference of dishonest intent which, the prosecution said, must be drawn from the facts they would prove.

Manion had pleaded not guilty to all counts and the trial had begun. Before this, however, James Geddy had applied for the Grievous Bodily Harm count to be severed and made the subject of a separate trial, but the prosecution had opposed this and the judge had ruled against him.

As things turned out, this proved to be a pyrrhic victory for the crown, since, when the time came, there was no Ricky Pitts to give evidence. It transpired that he had been warned by the police the previous evening to attend Court the following day, but had left his home in the middle of the night and disappeared. Intensive police efforts to find him were unsuccessful and the jury in Number 1 Court found themselves deprived of his evidence.

Unrecovered from this body blow to their case, the crown had next had to face a Mr Lusk who retired so far from his original evidence as to make it sound that Manion had done him a favour by accepting two large sums of money from him. As a result, it had been left to James Geddy in cross-examination merely to underscore Mr Lusk's reluctance to pull the trigger in his client's face.

As to the fourth count, the crown had proved a number of incontrovertible facts and said that Manion's dishonest intent was the only possible inference. Manion, of course, had denied any such dishonesty in the transaction in question.

James Geddy glanced at his watch. 'Time we got back into Court, Robin. So we'll have a shot at getting him out of the lot, shall we! The judge is bound to sling the G.B.H. and I think there's a very fair chance of his upholding my submission of no case on Counts Two and Three after Mr Lusk's performance in the box. He certainly ought to, but judges aren't always the lilywhite guardians of virginal justice the public likes to believe. Maybe because justice lost her virginity when first given into the charge of frail mortals. As for Count Four, I'll try and persuade him that it, too, is unworthy of any answer, but Peter Strange is certainly going to fight to hold him on something. The police must be hopping mad the way the case has gone.'

Robin nodded gravely. 'I imagine they suspect that Manion's responsible for Pitt's disappearance and for Lusk's watered down evidence.'

'I wouldn't have thought there was any doubt about it. Their imagining it, I mean,' he added drily.

When they arrived back in Court, Adrian Slatter was already there, leaning against the dock and talking to George Uppard, his chief clerk, a genial-looking tough among whose reputed duties was that of undertaking the firm's occasional extra-curricular activities. He turned to leave and gave Geddy a friendly nod. Robin received a knowing wink and smiled back. He and Slatter made a strange pair, but Robin supposed that, if you were a one-man firm and attracted clients as shady as so many of Slatter's, it was necessary to employ someone who could, so to speak, guard the shop when occasion required. At first he had been rather shocked by all he had heard about Adrian Slatter's practice, but since meeting him he had come round to the view that his services to the criminal community were almost those of some philanthropic organisation.

The judge entered and a few seconds later Manion came up the steps at the back of the dock and sat down with a prison officer at his side. Before doing so, however, he glanced quickly down to make sure that his counsel and solicitor were in their places. Robin had noticed how he did this every time. There was something impressive about the gesture, as though he would not hesitate to hold up the proceedings if one of them were missing. Some defendants are shrunken wretches, others faceless nonentities, others again dominant forces who manage to make their presence felt just by being there. Manion was one of these. He was of medium height, broad-shouldered with a rather square-shaped head. He had black hair brushed straight back, a wide thin mouth and a pair of eyes which never reflected any emotion, but which would suddenly focus on something with frightening intensity. All his movements were neat and extremely rapid.

The afternoon's proceedings had scarcely begun before he leaned over the edge of the dock and waved a small piece of folded paper at his solicitor. Slatter rose and put up his hand to take it. Robin watched idly to see whether he passed the note back to James Geddy. But he didn't. Instead, he tore it into small pieces which he placed in a neat pile beside his papers.

Robin suddenly realised that he was missing some of the witness's evidence and bent over his notebook with a faint feeling of guilt.

But somehow he found it difficult to concentrate that afternoon. He kept on thinking of Sheila and wondering if he would have an opportunity of speaking to her alone that evening. He hated having to conceal his feelings about her; hated, too, all the hole-in-the-corner measures he was obliged to adopt just to steal a furtive kiss. And then not always successfully. If only he could also be more sure of Sheila's exact feelings towards him. The present situation was becoming unbearable. He had enough to occupy his mind with trying to establish himself in his new profession, without the additional strain of a frustrated emotional entanglement.

Eventually Chief Superintendent Peters completed his evidence and Strange announced that that was the close of the prosecution's case. James Geddy rose to begin his submission, but paused when the judge and the clerk of the court went into a whispered huddle. The judge kept on glancing up at the clock as though to will it to stop.

'Mr Geddy,' he said after a final exchange with the clerk and a last dismissive look at the clock, 'I think we shall have to break off at this point as I have to interpose another matter which will occupy the rest of the afternoon. And I shan't be able to sit to-morrow morning so I'll adjourn this case until two o'clock to-morrow afternoon.'

'If your lordship pleases,' Geddy said and sat down, his tone indicating anything but pleasure on his own part.

A couple of minutes later, he and Robin and prosecuting counsel were outside the Court.

'Someone might have given us a bit of warning,' he remarked. 'Did you know he was going to do this, Peter?'

Strange shook his head. 'No, but I'll be quite glad to have to-morrow morning in Chambers. Anyway, I'm sure your submission will keep.'

'Oh, I'm not worried about my submission. It's just that this'll mean adding at least half a day on to the trial and I've got something specially fixed in the Court of Appeal on Friday.'

'So what, James. It's always happening. I've had no fewer than four of my cases listed to-day in different Courts. One just goes where the thunder rolls loudest and leaves one's clerk to sort out the rest.'

'I still don't have to approve the system whereby it happens.'

'System?' Strange echoed in mock surprise. 'Since when has system had any part in a barrister's life? It's just day-to-day semi-organised chaos.'

Robin always enjoyed the walk back to Chambers from the Old Bailey, even on a grey November's afternoon. Buses were full and pavements crowded as the first commuters made their way home and one had the feeling of being in the heart of things. There was always the chance of some new breathtaking glimpse of St Paul's in silhouette if you happened suddenly to glance behind you. And if you didn't, Fleet Street was there to stimulate the mind in a different way with its air of vibrant activity. To one who had first visited London at the edge of sixteen and who had only been living there for quite a short time, the whole atmosphere was charged with excitement, especially all those areas connected with the law.

He had short legs and had difficulty in keeping up with James Geddy who seemed to be able to keep going in a straight line while he, Robin, was for ever dodging round human and other obstacles.

But at last they turned down one of the alleys which fed the Temple like so many tributaries. Mulberry Court itself was tucked away at the end of an arched-over passage which provided its only entrance and egress. The tree which gave it its name stood in the middle of the small courtyard, heavily propped up with iron poles which had become almost part of it. There was a doorway on each of three of the courtyard's sides which led to sets of Chambers. These were numbers 2, 3 and 4 Mulberry Court. Number 4 was on the right-hand side as you emerged from the passage. There was no number 1, and there never had been to anyone's knowledge. The Temple's archives, moreover, were silent on this minor mystery.

Number 4 contained six sets of Chambers, James Geddy's being ground-floor left as you entered. As they passed through the doorway, Robin's eyes took in, as they always did, the panels bearing the names of those in the various sets. He hoped that his own might one day appear there as a full-blown tenant. Outside the entrance to each set, the names of those barristers in that particular set appeared once more, though this time in larger letters. Head of Chambers was Martin Ainsworth Q.C. whose name topped the list. James Geddy's was fifth, immediately below that of Anthea Rayner, the only female member of Chambers. Below Geddy's came five more names and at the bottom in slightly smaller letters appeared, 'Clerk: Mr D. Swingler.'

'I always think Donald's name ought to be in the largest letters of all,' James Geddy had once remarked to Robin. 'He's about the only indispensable person in Chambers.'

And this in a sense was true. Donald was one of the Temple's young clerks. When his predecessor had finally retired, it had been felt necessary to bring in someone young and energetic to try and repair the damage old John had wrought through his off-hand treatment of solicitors. The trouble was that he had become tired and lazy and though he 'clerked' the senior members of Chambers reasonably satisfactorily, he did very little for the younger members who eventually threatened to break away and set up elsewhere (there was more hope than practicality in their talk at the time) unless something was done. And so John was pensioned off and Donald, who had been the number two clerk for quite some time, was given the job.

The clerk's room was the usual half past four scene of activity when James Geddy and Robin arrived back. Donald appeared to be making two telephone calls at once and Sheila was typing an opinion as though her life depended on its completion. Of Stephen, the junior clerk, there was no immediate sign, but he suddenly appeared behind them carrying two mugs of tea.

'Who are those for?' Geddy asked, eyeing the tea with interest.

'One's for Mr Ainsworth, the other's for . . .' Stephen jerked his head in the direction of a nervous young man who was sitting very upright on a chair just inside the main door. 'He's come for a con with Miss Rayner, but the solicitor hasn't arrived yet,' Stephen whispered as he pushed his way past Geddy and Robin.

'Well, Mr Appleman and I would like some, too.'

'You're back early, sir, aren't you?'

'A bit. Judge had something else to deal with before the end of the day.'

'How much longer's Donald going to be on the phone?' Geddy asked, watching the clerk with an expression of admiration as he juggled with his two callers.

Stephen glanced at Donald, then shrugged. 'Could be some time, sir. He's trying to get one of Mr Ainsworth's cases swapped around and it's taking a bit of doing. There are three other silks involved.' James Geddy grunted. 'I'll tell him to come and have a word with you, sir, as soon as he's free.'

Geddy wandered off down the passage to his room, but Robin remained standing in the doorway watching Sheila. He wished she would look up from her typing, but she showed no signs of doing so. With luck, if she was as busy as this, she would be staying late this evening to finish her work. Sometimes she would be there after Donald and Stephen had gone.

'Hello, Robin, what sort of a day have you had?'

Robin turned to find David March behind him. David was a fellow-pupil in chambers, though not James Geddy's. He was the same age as Robin, but had a very different background. His father was a famous doctor and David had been to a fashionable school and then Oxford. At first, Robin had been on the defensive, but it had not been long before David's unaffected friendliness had persuaded him that he had nothing to fear on the score of social inequality.

'We're about to submit,' Robin replied, using the proprietorial 'we' that pupils often do when discussing their pupil-masters' cases.

'Do you think you'll get Manion out on a submission?'

'He's likely to be held on at least one count. And what about you? Where've you been today?'

'Middlesex Sessions this morning and Bow Street this afternoon. Both walk-overs,' he added with a grin. 'Philip's now gone off home with a cold.'

Philip Quant was David's pupil-master and next in seniority to James Geddy. He was a rather sardonic, schoolmasterish person whom Robin didn't like, though David said he was perfectly all right provided you made it plain that you didn't take him too seriously.

'Coming up to the Templar later?' David asked, at the same time casting a casual glance at the nervous young man who was still sitting bolt upright over by the door.

The Templar was one of the public houses in the area frequented by the Bar and the one most favoured by their Chambers.

Robin's gaze went back to Sheila before he replied.

'I expect so,' he said in a vague tone. 'I'd better go and find out whether James wants me for anything. I'll join you if I can.'

He went off down the passage as though he had suddenly

remembered an urgent appointment at the other end. David watched him with a small smile, then turning back to the clerks' room, where Donald was still on the telephone, he said hopefully, 'Any more biscuits? I didn't have any lunch to-day.'

Sheila stopped typing and looked over her shoulder at him. ''Fraid not. Miss Rayner raided the tin when she came in. I gather she also failed to get any lunch. But I'll buy some more on my way in to-morrow.'

David drifted away. Sheila was an attractive girl, as well as being an extremely competent typist, and everyone liked her. It was painfully obvious, however, that Robin was infatuated with her and that she didn't reciprocate his feelings, which would be embarrassing if she were not so obviously able to take care of the situation. Although not officially engaged, she was known to have a steady boy-friend who was also rumoured to be extremely jealous. He had turned up in Chambers once or twice to collect her, a tense, somewhat glowering young man whose response to any greeting was never anything more than a quick nod. But David reckoned this was probably due to his unease in a completely strange atmosphere. If he was of a jealous disposition, he would hardly welcome Sheila working in such a masculine atmosphere. One, moreover, with quite a few unattached and not unattractive males always around, who were additionally cloaked with all the proverbial glamour of a barrister's life. Poor old Sheila's boy-friend, David thought, it was a bit tough on him! But then it was up to him to persuade her to change her job if he minded that much.

David opened the door of Anthea Rayner's room and looked in.

'Hello,' he said hopefully, stepping inside.

'I'm about to start a con, David, so if you're merely looking for somewhere to gossip, you'll have to try elsewhere.'

Anthea Rayner wore her no-nonsense air like a cloak she never left off. She was in her mid-forties and of sufficiently solid build to cause any bag-snatcher to have second thoughts. Her dark hair was pulled back into a large bun in the nape of her neck and she dressed without exception in a black coat and skirt and white blouse. Only the material of her garb changed between winter and summer. She was a competent advocate and a particularly good prosecutor. She had the only other pupil in Chambers, Holly Childersley, who was terrified of her.

It was Holly who now gave David a nervous smile.

'Oh,' he said, 'I just wondered if you'd be coming up to the Templar later on.'

It was rare for Anthea to join them, but occasionally she did. 'I shan't be. I'm supposed to be going to a concert. I can't answer for Holly.' She gave her pupil a quizzical look.

'Yes, I'll see you there, David,' Holly said. 'Provided our con finishes in time,' she added hastily.

'It's jolly well going to finish in time,' Anthea Rayner declared firmly. 'It'll last no longer than it takes me to tell our lay client that he hasn't a hope in hell and has got to plead guilty. And that,' she added, 'is not going to take long.'

Holly smiled at her anxiously as though it were she who was about to be thrown to the judicial wolves.

'See you later then, Holly,' David said and wandered out of the room.

For the next hour or so, Chambers was the scene of quiet but intensive activity. A number of conferences with solicitors and lay clients were taking place in various rooms and in others people were catching up on the reading of briefs and the paper work which awaits most barristers after a day spent in Court. However, David March managed to find a couple of junior members of Chambers who were prepared to push back their chairs and join in a cosy exchange of 'shop' talk. Shortly before six o'clock, they decided to adjourn to the Templar. As they left, they popped their heads in to the clerks' room to say good night, but Donald was back on the phone again and Sheila was still furiously typing. Stephen had apparently gone.

About half an hour later, Robin, who had been hovering on and off in the vicinity of the clerks' room, made a carefully casual entrance after seeing Donald shoot along to Martin Ainsworth's room.

'Hello, Sheila, I was wondering if you'd care to come out and have a drink with me? On your way home, I mean.'

'I'm afraid I can't to-night. I'm just going now.'

'Oh ... well, I'll walk up to the bus stop with you.'

'Actually my boy-friend's waiting for me. He's got his car.'

'Perhaps to-morrow night then ...' But before he could complete the sentence, Sheila had hurried past him and the hand he had put out to touch her fell dispiritedly to his side. As it did so, he noticed that she had dropped one of the letters she had been carrying. Hurriedly he picked it up off the floor and chased after her. She was just getting into a red Austin mini when he reached her.

'Sheila,' he called out as he ran up to the car, 'Sheila, you dropped this letter.'

He saw the slightly cold expression of the young man in the driver's seat, then Sheila said, 'I wonder if you'd mind posting it for me ... Robin.'

His heart did a small leap. It was the first time she had addressed him by his Christian name. Normally, she was punctilious in her use of 'Mr Appleman this' or 'Mr Appleman that'.

The car spurted away, leaving Robin holding the letter as though it conveyed news of his instant knighthood. He decided to post it and go straight home without dropping in at the Templar.

About this time, James Geddy wandered in to Anthea Rayner's room to find her talking to Martin Ainsworth.

'I was just asking Anthea about her pupil,' Ainsworth explained.

'She's quite a bright girl, isn't she?' Geddy said.

Anthea snorted. 'Oh yes, she's quite intelligent, but who ever heard of a barrister called Holly?'

'I don't see that her Christian name need be any handicap at the Bar,' Ainsworth remarked in a tone of surprise. 'After all, they're not bandied about in Court, even in these progressive times. And for that matter, have you ever glanced down the list of judges in the Law List? Some of them have got some pretty curious names tucked away in the middle.' He smiled broadly. 'Miss Justice Holly Childersley, I think that it sounds rather good!'

'I confess that I don't exactly see her as a potent advocate,' Geddy said.

'Nor I,' Anthea observed. 'Her only success would be in front of all-male juries.'

Both men laughed and Geddy said, 'She's certainly an extremely pretty girl. I don't imagine she'll remain unmarried for very long.'

'It's sometimes positively embarrassing the attention she attracts in Court,' Anthea said. 'I think it would have been much better if she'd been pupilled to a man.'

'I don't see that that would have diminished the attention she receives,' Ainsworth said with a wink at James Geddy.

'No, but it would have made me feel less like the matron of a Victorian reformatory with one of her more winsome delinquent girls in tow.' She looked at Geddy. 'What about swapping pupils, James? I get on rather well with your Robin Appleman. He'd soon lose all the chips off his shoulders if he went around with me.'

'Chips?' Ainsworth echoed. 'What chips has he got on his shoulders?'

'I think he has a bit of an inferiority complex,' Geddy replied thoughtfully. 'Humble background, pulled himself up by his own bootstrings, unsophisticated by present standards, that sort of thing. But he's very conscientious and I think he's going to be all right, if he can overcome his tendency to turn up in Court looking as though he'd got caught up in a demonstration on the way.'

'Now you mention it, he is faintly scruffy, isn't he?' Ainsworth observed.

'But not unattractive,' Anthea said in a tone which

bordered on the smug. Both men looked at her sharply. 'Oh, I don't mean that I've fallen for the poor young man,' she added robustly. 'But I'm not so sure about Sheila.'

'Sheila! Our Sheila, do you mean?'

'Yes, our Sheila. Of course, men never notice these things! But Robin Appleman never misses an opportunity of popping into the clerks' room, especially if Sheila's in there on her own.'

'And what does Sheila think about that?' Geddy asked.

'I don't think she's decided yet.'

'How do you know all this, Anthea?'

'By keeping my eyes and ears open, the way you both do in Court. I do it in Chambers as well.'

'Well, I'm not sure that I approve,' Ainsworth said, after a pause in which both men had pondered their colleague's last remark.

'Why on earth not?' Anthea asked. 'Good heavens, he's not actually knocking her off behind the switchboard!'

'That may come,' Geddy added.

'I'm not bothered on moral grounds of that sort,' Ainsworth said, 'though I wouldn't want it going on behind the switchboard as you picturesquely put it, Anthea. It's just that Sheila's the best Chambers typist we've ever had and Robin Appleman is, so to speak, only here on sufferance and it would be maddening if we were to lose Sheila on his account, either because she wanted to get away from him or in order to become Mrs Appleman.'

'Has anyone else spotted this incipient romance?'

'Holly has, and I imagine David March, as well. You'd expect his fellow-pupils to know.'

'David March seems a good egg,' Ainsworth remarked, which brought their conversation to a close.

Shortly afterwards, all three of them left Chambers and James Geddy, who lived in Kensington, gave Anthea a lift home. She had a small flat not very far from where he and his wife and three children occupied a four-storey Victorian house.

Westwards along the Strand, they passed within a hun-

dred yards of the offices of Finster, Slatter & Co., Solicitors
and Commissioners for Oaths, which were just off one of
the narrow streets plunging towards the Embankment. Mr
Finster had passed into an alcoholic oblivion seven or eight
years before and from that, after a short time, into final
oblivion, so that the use of the plural to describe the firm
was inaccurate. However, the name remained and there was
still far too much wear in the brass plate to warrant a fresh
one.

The offices were reached up a narrow staircase from
street level and comprised five rooms, which led off the
small grimy entrance lobby. Each door had a panel of
frosted glass with the room's designation painted in black
letters on the outside. These were: Mr Adrian Slatter,
Managing Clerk, Clerks and Typists. There were three
clerks in addition to the managing clerk and five typists,
one of whom also minded the switchboard and another who
acted as Adrian Slatter's secretary.

At this particular moment, the firm's principal was the
only person in. He had for some time just been sitting
brooding at his desk, biting nervously at the skin at the
edge of his thumbnail.

It had been a tiring day in Court and now there was so
much work on his desk that it seemed pointless even to
begin. Indeed, he had no intention of making any start on it
this evening. It would just have to wait. Normally, of
course, he wouldn't waste his time instructing Counsel in
Court, he would send along one of his clerks. But Frank
Manion expected to see his solicitor there all the time and
Frank Manion was not the sort of client you crossed. But,
by God, it was going to cost him something in terms of
actual money!

The phone on his desk suddenly began ringing – when
the girls left an outside line was always switched through to
his office – and he rested his hand on the receiver for several
seconds before picking it up.

'Hello.' His tone was cautious.

'Is that Mr Slatter?' the voice was male. Rough, uneducated male.

'Who wants him?'

'Look, Mr Slatter, I'm speaking for Gashy Paynter. 'E's just been picked up. 'E's at the nick now. You'd better get along there quick.'

A small bubble of anger exploded inside Adrian Slatter's brain.

'Who the bloody hell do you think you're giving orders to? If Paynter's been arrested, that's too bad. I'm not rushing to his side at this hour of the evening. So you can hop back to the station and tell him that from me.' There was a silence at the other end apart from heavy breathing. 'What's he been arrested for, anyway?' he asked.

'That post-office job at Woolwich,' the voice replied, as though surprised that the question had been necessary. And indeed it had not, since Slatter had known that the police were after Paynter for that particular job.

'Is he at Woolwich Police Station?'

'S'right.'

'I'll speak to the officer in charge on the phone, but nothing's going to take me out to Woolwich to-night, I'll tell you that.'

'Gashy's going to be upset.'

Slatter dropped the receiver, rather than spit out the obscenity which formed on his lips. It was insufferable being spoken to in that way and treated as though you were at the willing beck and call of every crook in London. He was seething with anger again. It was happening far too often. Some of them seemed to think they owned you . . .

After a time, he managed to bring himself to phone the police station and left a message to the effect that there'd be someone at Court the next morning to represent Paynter, though he would not be able to be there himself. It then required a number of further phone calls to make the necessary arrangements.

It was eight o'clock by the time he had finished. Then pulling a small, red address book from his waistcoat pocket, he thumbed carefully through the pages to the end and back again. Finally he lit on one page and leaned forward to reach for the telephone. He dialled a number and waited. It seemed it was not going to be answered and his brow had begun to crease in a petulant frown when he heard a voice at the other end.

'Jackie?'

'Yes.'

'Adrian.'

'Well, well, how's my lawyer boy?'

'Wanting company.'

'Well, that fits in with my plans, too.'

'I'll be over right away.'

He jumped up from his desk and a few seconds later was locking the street door behind him.

Life was not so bad after all.

II

Robin Appleman had a small furnished flat above a baker's shop not far from Lots Road Power Station. The furniture in it was adequate, but no more, and it was certainly not a place where he wished to entertain friends. Not that he had formed any real friendships since coming to London. He had always been something of a loner and never minded going off on his own – to a cinema or a museum or just for a walk. But his basic problem was money and would continue to be that until he began earning. It was for this reason that he had decided to seek a pupillage in predominantly criminal Chambers, since, thanks to 'legal aid' it was much easier to get started at the criminal than the civil Bar. Nevertheless his pupillage had to run twelve months, for the first six of which he was not permitted to appear in Court on his own, which, in effect, was a bar on earning any money.

All of this meant that he was forced to live on a very

tight budget and there was little over after he had paid the rent of his modest abode, his travelling expenses which were invariably more than he had allowed for, and for his food. He usually ate in the evenings at a small café near the baker's shop where you could get the usual run of things 'with chips'.

It bothered him faintly that he had neither the facilities nor the resources to return hospitality, though he was aware that those who *had* entertained him did not expect him to reciprocate. This was especially true of the Geddys who had asked him to dinner and Sunday lunch once or twice and of David March who had invited him to meals at the flat which he shared with a brother who was a medical student.

The financial pinch apart, however, he was quite happy in a quietly controlled fashion. One way and another, he managed.

On the day after he had posted the letter for Sheila, he rose somewhat later than usual. The Manion trial was not being resumed until after lunch and James Geddy had announced that he would be working at home all the morning and would be going to Court straight from there, so this left Robin to his own devices.

It was not without some cunning that he timed his arrival in Chambers for eleven o'clock. It was almost certain that everyone would be in Court. But, more important, it was probable that both Donald and Stephen would also be out, either in attendance at a Court where one of the senior members of Chambers was appearing or coffee-housing with other Chambers clerks. This meant that Sheila would be holding the fort alone. At any rate, he hoped that would be the position, and was, in due course, rewarded to find that it was so.

'Hello, Sheila, you in sole charge this morning?' he enquired in a tone of undisguised pleasure.

'You made me jump,' she said, swivelling round on her typist's chair. 'I wasn't expecting you in. Yes, Donald's gone over to see someone in the Court of Appeal office and

Stephen's at Sessions. They'll both be back in about half an hour.'

Robin nodded, though he was in no hurry for their return.

'I posted your letter, by the way.'

'What letter?' Sheila looked puzzled.

'The one you dropped when you were leaving last night.'

'Oh ... oh yes, of course. Thank you, Mr Appleman.'

'Why don't you call me Robin? You did last night.'

She looked at him thoughtfully for a few seconds.

'I can't call you Robin in Chambers. Donald wouldn't approve.'

'Surely you can when no one's about?'

'That never happens.'

'It's happening now.'

'Yes, but normally it doesn't happen. It's the first time you've ever come into Chambers on your own in the middle of the morning. Have you come to pick up Mr Geddy's papers?'

Robin didn't care for the prosaic channel into which the conversation had suddenly become diverted. On the other hand, he wasn't sure how to get it out again.

'I thought something might have come in for him which he'd want at the Bailey this afternoon,' he said stupidly. 'Has Mr Slatter phoned by any chance?'

'Not to my knowledge. Was he supposed to?'

'No, but I thought he might have. About the Manion case, I mean.'

Sheila shook her head. 'Well, I must get on with my work. I've got enough to keep me here a month.'

'Does that mean you'll be working late this evening?'

'I shouldn't be at all surprised.'

Sheila turned back to her typewriter, but Robin continued to hover in the doorway.

'Does your boy-friend come and pick you up every evening?'

She answered without looking round. 'No, it depends where he's working. He's a sales rep for a magazine group.

25

He has to travel quite a bit.'

'Abroad?'

'Just around the home counties.'

'What's his name?'

'Alan. Alan Dixon.'

'Are you engaged?'

She gave a curious sort of half laugh. 'No, we're not engaged.'

It seemed that she might be about to add something further, but the small switchboard chose that moment to show Chambers had a caller. Sheila leaned across and put in a plug.

Robin waited hopefully, but it was soon apparent that Sheila was in no hurry to dispose of the caller. He gathered that it was Donald's wife. At all events, it was someone whom Sheila addressed as Janet and he knew that that was the name of their chief clerk's wife. Further confirmation came in the enquiries after Jamie and Nicholas, which were the names of Donald's two small sons.

He drifted off to James Geddy's room, saw that there was nothing new on his table and decided to make his way to the Old Bailey, particularly as he heard the outside door open and close, followed by sounds of Donald or Stephen. There was nothing to be gained by remaining in Chambers any longer, though the decision to depart served only to increase the feeling of frustration which had settled on him.

It was only twelve o'clock when he reached the Old Bailey and he spent the next hour sitting in one of the Courts listening to a fraud case of unimaginable boredom. Every flat surface was covered with documents, the jury gave the impression of having drifted into a fitful trance and even the judge appeared to have difficulty in keeping his mind on the witness's evidence. It was an accountant who was in the box and he seemed faintly amused by his awareness of the embracing tedium of his evidence as he patiently explained the complexities of some balance sheet.

Robin decided to stay and listen in the hope that he would learn something about the conduct of a complicated fraud case, but, in the event, his mind also drifted away into less arid pastures and he left Court feeling rather as he used to at the end of a Latin lesson at school.

He had a quick lunch and arrived outside Number 1 Court a good ten minutes before the resumption of business. At least, he would avoid any reproaches to-day.

George Uppard, Adrian Slatter's managing clerk, was talking earnestly to a huge, brawny, pot-bellied man whom Robin had seen several times in the course of the trial. He was a friend of Manion's and the two often exchanged covert signs of recognition as Manion was leaving the door to go down to the cells beneath the Court. The fat man made jabbing gestures at Uppard with his right forefinger when he spoke. Uppard would listen intently and then reply with equal vigour before the onset of the next series of jabs. Robin was unable to hear what they were saying and something in their manner kept him at a distance.

'Robin!' He turned at the sound of his name to see James Geddy about to go into Court.

'I've just been having a word with Peter Strange,' Geddy said as Robin joined him, 'and he's not in the mood to concede anything. He's going to try and hold Manion on everything, except the G.B.H.'

'But surely the judge must uphold your submission on Counts Two and Three,' Robin said vehemently.

Geddy shrugged. 'Judges can be as unpredictable as juries and old Tyler is not the sort to let on which way his thoughts are going.' He paused. 'Shall I tell you my test of a good judge, Robin? He's the one who, when the trial's over, leaves you feeling that you had a fair run for your money regardless of whether you won or lost the case.' He cocked a sardonic eye at Robin. 'And there aren't all that number of whom one can say that!'

'Is Mr Justice Tyler among them?'

'Not really, though he's not as much of an outcast as some others.' He removed the piece of pink tape from round his brief and began to spread out his papers. 'However, I still think we must throw everything we've got into this submission. I don't fancy Manion as a witness.'

'But Mr Slatter said he'd be a good witness.'

'That's the trouble, I'm afraid he'll be too good! I don't want to sound too cynical, Robin, but it's next to impossible for someone like Frank Manion to receive a fair trial. A truly fair trial. His reputation is too widely known and the ordinary man in the street is getting a bit tired of the Manions in our midst. So given half a chance, they'll down him. And all one'll be able to say afterwards is that he was unlucky to be convicted on such evidence. Unlucky because, on balance, he ought to have been acquitted and unluckier still because the verdict is not so perverse as to warrant any prospect of reversal on appeal.'

'Perhaps the judge will misdirect the jury on law,' Robin said hopefully.

James Geddy grinned. 'Certainly, there's always a chance of that in this splendid lottery known as justice.'

A few seconds later, the judge made his entry, followed by Manion who came up the steps into the dock. He cast his usual quick glance around before sitting down.

'Yes, Mr Geddy, I believe you have a submission to make?'

'I have, my lord.'

'Will it assist you if I say I propose to direct the jury to return a verdict of Not Guilty on Count One?'

'That does, indeed, assist me and I am much obliged to your lordship.'

'But there are other matters on which you wish to submit?'

'There are, my lord. I wish to submit that there is no case to go to the jury on the remaining three counts of the indictment.'

'I see. In that event, it would clearly be advisable that the jury should retire to their room.'

'I agree, my lord.'

Mr Justice Tyler turned towards the jury-box. 'Members of the jury, as you have just heard, defending Counsel wishes to make a submission in law to me and it is usual for such submissions to be heard in the absence of the jury in case anything is said which might prejudice the future course of the trial. In the event, that is to say,' he added in a parchment-dry tone, 'of the trial having a future course . . .'

The jury now filed out of Court with the passive obedience expected of those press-ganged into the service of justice. In doing so, two tripped, one dropped his spectacles and someone's hat suddenly appeared at a female juror's feet like a ball from a rugger scrum.

When the door had closed behind the last juror, Mr Justice Tyler gave James Geddy a small nod and he began his submission. As he did so, Manion leaned forward over the edge of the dock and attracted Adrian Slatter's attention with yet another small folded note.

The solicitor rose and took it from him, though with a clearly reproving look. Robin sympathised. It was very disconcerting for James Geddy to have someone bobbing about just in front of him when he was addressing the judge and it was, for that reason, embarrassing to Adrian Slatter. Robin added his own reproving glance, but Manion was far too intent on making sure that his solicitor read the note to take any notice. Slatter, however, merely slipped it among his papers and hunched himself over the table in an attitude of concentrated endeavour. Manion cast him a final unrequited glance before slowly sitting back in his own chair. Earlier in the trial, one of the prison officers in the dock with him had tried to make him sit down as soon as he had passed a note, but Manion had curtly shaken off the man's hand and had thereafter been allowed free rein in the ungainly method of communication dictated by their respective positions.

James Geddy's submission lasted just under half an hour and was followed by prosecuting counsel's reply which was somewhat shorter.

As Peter Strange sat down, Mr Justice Tyler cleared his throat and said, 'I uphold your submission on Counts Two and Three, Mr Geddy, but am against you on Count Four.

29

Let the jury now be brought back into Court.'

Adrian Slatter turned round in his chair to speak to Geddy. 'I take it Manion will be in the box for the rest of the afternoon?'

'Yes, and for at least half to-morrow as well, I would guess. Strange will certainly cross-examine him for quite a while and I have a fair amount of ground to cover with him just on Count Four.' The last juror was now back in his place. James Geddy rose and said, 'I call my client, my lord.' He glanced towards the dock where Manion sprang up briskly, straightened his tie, smoothed the front of his jacket and turned to make his way to the witness-box, escorted by one of the prison officers.

Robin opened his notebook at a clean page, wrote, 'Manion: examination-in-chief' at the top, underlined the words carefully, and waited with his pen poised. James Geddy faced the witness across the well of the Court, his right hand rested on the back of his seat almost touching Robin's notebook. It was a hairy hand and Robin found himself wondering exactly how many hairs there were. Then he concentrated his mind on the task of making the fullest possible note of Manion's evidence.

Manion's voice was soft and as expressionless as his eyes. He had not gone far before the judge declared in a small display of judicial petulance that he was sure the jury were unable to hear his evidence.

Robin had already noticed this trait among judges of ascribing their own difficulties of hearing to the jury, though in the present instance it was probably justified.

Manion gave Mr Justice Tyler a cool, unembarrassed look and apologised rather as though he was excusing his lordship's outburst.

It was towards the end of the afternoon while he was still giving his evidence that Manion asserted that confirmation of something he had just said could be found in a document which he had sent to his solicitor. There followed one of those pauses in which everyone's interest suddenly shifts.

The judge and prosecuting counsel looked at James

Geddy, who, in turn, stared at the back of his instructing solicitor who was feverishly sorting through a mass of paper in front of him.

'If your lordship will forgive me a moment ...' Geddy murmured and bent forward to give Adrian Slatter a small prod in the shoulder blade. 'What is this document? I've not seen it, have I?'

Slatter swivelled round on his chair. 'I don't seem to have it here. I'll have to look for it in the office.'

'What is it, anyway?'

'I'm not sure what he's referring to.'

'You'd better find out from him when we adjourn.' James Geddy's tone was chilly. He did not like the sudden feeling that his trousers might be about to come down. 'I apologise, my lord,' he said as he straightened up, 'the document in question doesn't appear to be in Court at the moment, but I hope to have further instructions about it by to-morrow morning.'

'Very well.' Mr Justice Tyler sounded bored by the whole business.

At four o'clock meaningful glances were cast at the Court clock, but the judge appeared not to notice. James Geddy concluded that Mr Justice Tyler must have decided to sit a bit later to compensate for the lost morning and had just begun to embark on a fresh facet of Manion's evidence when the judge announced that the Court would adjourn until half past ten the next morning. It was then five past four.

Robin threw down his pen and rubbed his fingers which had become stiff from writing. Stephen, the junior clerk, suddenly appeared and began gathering up James Geddy's scattered papers. Manion was ignoring the prison officers' signs that he should return to the cells and was leaning over the edge of the dock flicking his fingers at his solicitor who was shuffling his own papers into his brief case.

'I'll come down and have a word with you in a minute,' Slatter said impatiently.

Manion seemed about to say something, but turned and

allowed himself to be escorted down the narrow stairs at the rear of the dock.

'Now what about this document he was talking about?' Geddy enquired.

'I'll find it and send it round to Chambers,' Slatter said. 'He's sent me so much bumph, I'll have to sort through the lot. I'm awfully sorry, Mr Geddy, but I thought I'd included everything that mattered in your brief.'

'I'm sure you did, but I'd better have a look at whatever it is, seeing that he has referred to it in his evidence. Whether or not it confirms what he's told the Court remains to be seen. At the moment, the inference of fraud remains so that anything that helps to provide an innocent explanation for his conduct is obviously important to his case.'

'Quite.' Slatter nodded gravely.

'On the other hand if this document really does help towards that end, you'd have spotted it and would've let me have a copy, so my hopes are not very high.' He sighed. 'Witnesses seldom know what's important or unimportant in the way of evidence. Clients even less so.'

Slatter smiled wanly. Robin thought he looked washed out. His was not a role to be envied.

'I'm sure I shall be able to dig it out and I'll send it round straight away,' he said.

'The only thing about that,' Geddy replied, 'is that I'm going off home almost immediately. It's my fourteen-year-old son's birthday and we're going out to celebrate and I promised to get back early.'

'I can wait for it in Chambers,' Robin said quickly, 'and then I'll put it through your letter-box on my own way home.'

'Are you sure you can conveniently do that, Robin?'

'Yes, easily.'

'Fine. Well, that's fixed that. You'd better go below and see Manion before they take him back to Brixton.'

Slatter closed his bulging brief-case slowly as though to put off as long as possible the moment of unwanted confrontation.

'Don't hurry for me,' Robin said in an aside not intended for Geddy's ears, 'I'll stay on in Chambers until it comes. I'm not in any rush to get away.'

Slatter nodded. 'I'll send someone round with it as soon as I can.'

'Well, as I say, no hurry as far as I'm concerned.'

Stephen had brought James Geddy's car to the Old Bailey in order that Geddy could drive straight home. His normal routine, when in a case at the Old Bailey, was to drive to the Temple where he had a parking permit and leave it there until he drove home again in the evening after finishing in Chambers.

After Stephen had shown him where he'd parked the car, he and Robin set off for Chambers on foot.

'Enjoying things, are you, Mr Appleman?' he enquired cheerfully, as they walked down the short street which had given its name to the Court.

'Tremendously. I think I'm pretty lucky being Mr Geddy's pupil. Also they're such friendly Chambers.'

'I guess they are. Some are right dumps. And though perhaps it's not for me to say so, Donald's a bloody good clerk. I regard myself as lucky learning under him.'

'What happens later on, do you go off to another set of Chambers as number one clerk?'

'That's the idea if everything works out. Mind you, I wouldn't want to go just anywhere, because, as I said a moment ago, some Chambers are real dumps with a few old dears trying to scrape a living. I reckon the Bar's the worst profession of any for hangers-on. The Temple's choc with them. The sort who try and make you believe their practice never takes them below the Court of Appeal, when you know perfectly well they'd leap at a brief marked five at some Magistrates Court.'

'Rather pathetic really! I hope I never become one of them.'

'I like to think you'd have the sense to get out if you couldn't make a go of private practice.' Stephen paused. 'I'm afraid I'm talking a bit out of turn. I'm sorry. After all, you are a barrister. I'm only a barrister's clerk. Well, not even that, a barrister's clerk's assistant. Of course,' he went on, as though changing back into top gear, 'most people in my position hope to get the number one job when the clerk retires. But the snag there is that Donald is only six years older than I am. However, it's too early to worry that far ahead and I certainly shan't look around for anything else for several years yet.'

They turned down one of the narrow passages leading off Fleet Street into the Temple. Just before they reached Mulberry Court, Stephen said, 'I'd be grateful, Mr Appleman, if you'd not repeat anything I've said. It's not a good thing to get a reputation for indiscretion. At least, not when you've still got only one foot on the ladder.'

Robin nodded. 'I shan't say anything.' If Stephen had not talked so hard, he had been going to bring the conversation delicately round to his own prospects after the completion of his pupillage. It was a topic which considerably occupied his thoughts, though one to which, as he knew, Stephen would have been able to contribute little, apart from some platitudes. It was as well that the opportunity had not come up. It would have only been like picking at a spot.

When they reached Chambers, Stephen immediately dived into the clerks' room where Donald was inevitably on the telephone. There was no sign of Sheila and Robin felt his heart drop two inches. Surely she could not have gone home already ... not when he had given himself a legitimate reason for staying on late in Chambers solely in the hope of having her company. At that moment he heard someone behind him and turned to find her coming along the passage with a cup of tea in each hand. His face lit up.

'Shall I carry one of those for you?'

'No, I can manage, thanks. Do you want a cup, Mr Appleman?'

'I'd love one.'

'Have one of these then.'

Robin experienced a feeling of slight let-down as he accepted the cup from her. He had hoped for a couple of delicious minutes squashed in the cupboardlike recess in which tea was brewed. Instead he was left to take his tea along to James Geddy's room.

Most of the rooms in Chambers were shared by two, if not three, people, but Geddy had one to himself. It was a small room with a long narrow window which provided an oblique view of the gardens and distant river. In the centre was a green leather-topped desk of modest proportions and over against one wall a table covered with briefs, some of them vast mountains of paper, others no more than the size of a slenderly folded magazine.

Robin normally used one end of this table for working, but, having the room to himself for once, decided to sit in his pupil-master's winged swivel chair. It was an impressive chair, very much a throne compared with the others in the room and was a natural focal point of attention when Geddy held conferences with solicitors and lay clients.

Geddy made almost a fetish of keeping his desk free of papers, except when he was actually working on them and its only adornments were a silver inkwell, a heavy jade paperweight, and a silver paperknife which was a reproduction eighteenth-century meat skewer. This had been given him by a previous pupil on completion of his year's pupillage.

Robin was mildly surveying these articles as he swivelled soothingly to and fro, when the door opened and David March looked in. His face immediately broke into a grin and Robin blushed.

'Trying it out for size, Robin?' he enquired.

'Hmm! Some hope! If any of us get offered a tenancy in Chambers it won't be I. You're much more likely to be asked to stay on.'

'Why?'

Robin shrugged. He had a wary, defensive expression. 'Your face fits better.'

'That's balls, Robin, and you know it.'

'You've got the right sort of background. That still counts for something at the Bar.'

'That's another load of old codswallop. If any of us gets offered a place, it'll be the one who, they believe, will bring in the work. It probably won't be poor old Holly, because there's still some prejudice against girls at the Bar. One's always hearing how hard they find it to get into good Chambers...'

'Exactly, prejudice!' Robin broke in bitterly.

'There's certainly none against you,' David said in a tone of slight exasperation. 'For God's sake, Robin! I defy you to name a single incident, since we've been pupils, which has shown that I'm more favourably looked on than you are. You can't name one!'

'You find it much easier to get on with people than I do,' Robin said sullenly.

'Why have you got such a bloody great chip on your shoulder all of a sudden?'

'It isn't all of a sudden.'

David realised that this was true enough, though it didn't generally show quite as starkly as it was doing at this moment. Robin certainly made it very difficult for anyone to like him when he was in such an abrasively self-deprecating mood. And why was he? David tried to think back to what had induced the mood. Surely it couldn't have been brought on because he had discovered him sitting in Geddy's chair with that dreamy proprietorial air and had pulled his leg about it. But you never knew with these moody, introspective types. Sometimes it required less than the flutter of a leaf to throw them out of sorts. The only thing to do was to change the subject briskly and this he was about to do when Robin went on.

'Oh, I know everyone's very friendly on the surface, but that makes it all the more obvious.'

'Makes what all the more obvious?' David's tone was one of renewed exasperation.

'That I come from a different background.'

'What the hell's that got to do with anything!'

'You know perfectly well what it's got to do with it. It's because you do know that you make that sort of comment.'

David shook his head wearily.

'Come and have a drink.'

Robin shook his head peremptorily. 'I have to wait for some papers that Adrian Slatter's sending round.'

'Is that *all* you're waiting for?' David's tone was more snide than he had intended, but he had been stung by Robin's abrupt rejection of his olive branch.

'What do you mean by that?'

'Oh, this sudden enthusiasm for hanging around Chambers...'

Robin flushed angrily. 'I don't know what you mean.'

'Well, you'd better watch it, boy,' David said nastily, 'I understand she has a very jealous boy-friend.'

Before Robin could make any reply, he departed, closing the door noisily behind him. Back in his own pupil-master's room, he sat down and tried to concentrate his mind on the set of papers he had been reading a short time before.

Philip Quant glanced at him covertly. A few seconds later he said, 'Was it you slamming doors just now?'

'Sorry! I didn't actually mean to slam it.' David was still feeling put out over the whole silly incident and certainly had no desire to discuss it with a senior member of Chambers. Unfortunately, as he was aware, Philip Quant took an almost perverted pleasure in ferreting out the Temple's intrigues and politickings. And the nearer to home, the better!

'If I may say so with respect, David, you look as though door-slamming is just the sort of mood you're in. What's provoked you?'

'Nothing.'

'Or perhaps I should have asked who's provoked you?'

David looked up, his expression worried and unhappy. 'If you must know, I allowed myself to be provoked and now I feel a heel.'

'Because you think you were mean to your fellow-pupil? Perhaps I should be more specific, to your fellow-*male-*

pupil.'

'Yes.'

'And were you mean to him? As opposed to *thinking* you were mean to him?'

'I don't know. But either way I still feel a heel.'

'Very honourable of you, my dear David. But you have my sympathy.'

'Why?'

'Because Robin Appleman can be a very tiresome and irritating person at times.'

David glanced at Philip Quant with an expression of surprise and shock. Surprise because he hadn't imagined that his pupil-master had had enough contact with Robin to form such a judgment. Shock because it embarrassed him to hear Quant refer to a fellow-pupil in such opprobrious terms.

Quant met his glance with a hard, glittering expression. 'Don't look so shocked, David. I've already let it be known that, if we do have a vacancy when the time comes, Robin certainly won't receive my vote.'

'I like him,' David said, almost defiantly.

'Fine!' He paused and his expression changed. 'Let me just finish what I'm doing and then we'll go up to the Templar.'

'Right.' David's tone was unenthusiastic. Embarrassment had given way to a puzzled and uneasy feeling. It was almost as if some bad spirit were abroad in Chambers that evening.

Twenty minutes later, they were ready to leave. Quant stuck his head round the clerks' door to say good night. Donald was alone in the room and obviously also on the verge of departure.

'Cheque here for you, sir. Just come in,' he said cheerfully.

'Who from?'

'Smithson and Peacock.'

'Didn't know they owed me any money!'

'Case of Cunliffe.'

'Still doesn't ring a bell.'

'Didn't with me either, sir. I've just looked it up in the book. Drugs case at Maidstone Quarter Sessions.'

'But that was over a year ago!'

Donald nodded. 'I'm afraid they're not very quick payers. Also it'd slipped my notice that they hadn't paid or I'd have been on their tail.'

'How much?'

Donald picked up a cheque from his desk. 'Thirty-six pounds and seventy-five pence.'

Quant accepted the cheque and put it in his wallet. 'Mr March and I are just off. Has everyone left now?'

'There's only Mr Appleman here. He's waiting for some papers which Slatter's are sending round for Mr Geddy. And Sheila'll be back in a minute, she's just popped out to buy some sandwiches as she's got a couple of hours work she wants to finish.'

Philip Quant raised a sardonic eyebrow. 'Sheila and Mr Appleman left alone in Chambers, is that prudent?'

Donald smiled. 'I'm sure Sheila can look after herself all right.'

'That, if I may say so, has nothing whatsoever to do with prudence.'

At that moment, the door of Geddy's room opened and Robin came along the passage.

'Ah, Robin, you're just in time to come up to the Templar with David and myself,' Quant said in a hearty tone.

'I'm afraid I can't. I've got to stay on in Chambers for some papers Slatter's sending round for James.'

'You don't have to wait here. Come and have a drink and call back for them later.'

'I think I'd better hang on.'

'What on earth for? Sheila'll be here and she can take them in. Come and have a drink!'

David moved across to the outer door, embarrassed by such a merciless piece of needling. He had had no idea that Quant had formed such a strong dislike of Robin and could not for the life of him think what had occasioned it.

'No, I think I'll wait,' Robin said in a quietly determined tone.

Philip Quant shrugged. 'Oh, well, if we can't lure you, we can't. Good night, Donald.'

'Good night, Mr Quant. Good night, Mr March,' Donald sang out as the two men left.

Robin licked his lips and let out an imperceptible sigh, as at an ordeal ended.

'You just off, too, Donald?' he said.

Donald nodded. 'Yes, I'm just waiting for Sheila to get back. She's gone out to buy some sandwiches.'

'Oh, she hasn't finished, then?' There was a plain note of relief in his tone.

'She's got three Opinions and a couple of indictments to type. All of them promised for to-morrow morning.'

'Anything I can do to help since I have to be here?'

'Nothing, Mr Appleman, except keep out of her way,' Donald said crisply.

Robin looked at him sharply, but the clerk had turned his attention to the row of fee books he kept on a shelf above his desk. There was one for each member of Chambers and he took down Philip Quant's.

Robin went back to Geddy's room and closed the door. He glanced at his watch. It was a few minutes after half past six.

Sheila would be back soon and then Donald would go. He hoped Adrian Slatter's clerk was not already on his way with the papers. He had made it clear that he was ready to wait for them however late it might be.

He must have drifted away in a reverie, because the next thing he knew was that the door had opened and Sheila stood there. She said, 'I've just had a phone call from Mr Slatter. He's found the documents Mr Geddy wants and is sending George Uppard round with them. He'll be here in about half an hour or so. Meanwhile he apologises for the delay.'

She shut the door quickly before Robin could say anything. He glanced at his watch again. Only five minutes had passed since his last look.

He braced his shoulders against the back of James Geddy's swivel chair and stretched out his arms luxuriously.

It was in the same chair that he was found the next morning, though now pinned in a stiff, ungainly pose of violent death.

III

There are probably more formally well-dressed men to be seen in the City of London than in any comparable acreage elsewhere in the world. And of them all, it is doubtful whether there was one more consistently well turned-out than Detective Chief Superintendent Roy Roffey of the City of London Police. Beside him, even the directors of merchant banks and the senior partners of important stock-broking firms were apt to hide their cuffs or straighten their socks.

Robin's body had been found about half an hour before Chief Superintendent Roffey reached headquarters in Old Jewry that morning and the police machine had already been put into motion by the time he had hung up his bowler hat and umbrella and laid the carefully folded *Times* (folded at the 'leader' page) on his desk.

Almost immediately his phone rang and he was asked to go along to the Assistant Commissioner's room. In the temporary absence of the Commander, C.I.D., the Assistant Commissioner was himself overseeing the C.I.D.

'There's been a murder in the Temple,' the A.C. said without ceremony as he entered. 'A young barrister named Robin Appleman has been found dead at 4 Mulberry Court. Stabbed in the throat.' The A.C. gave him a hard stare. 'As you know, murders within the City are as rare as sunny days in January and it's a question of whether we ought not to ask the Yard for assistance.'

Chief Superintendent Roffey frowned as though at a tasteless remark.

'I don't see why, sir.'

'I thought that would be your reply.'

'The Yard may have more experience of investigating murders than we have, but that doesn't mean they have a monopoly of expertise.'

The A.C. looked thoughtful for a moment, then said briskly, 'Very well, I'll square it with the Commissioner. Meanwhile, you'd better get along there straight away. Who'll you take?'

'Detective Sergeant Chisett, sir.'

'Very well, find him and go.'

'I suppose I'd best call on the Treasurer of his Inn first.'

'What on earth for? Anyway, Treasurers of Inns are judges and the like. You won't find them sitting about the premises at this hour of the day.'

'The Temple's private property, sir, owned by the Inner and Middle Temples. I'm not quite sure which has jurisdiction over Mulberry Court.'

'Nor am I. Since you mention it, I suppose some sort of protocol approach may be required. Anyway, you get along there now and I'll sort that little problem out while you're on your way.'

The A.C. smiled grimly to himself as Roffey went out of the room. He could just see his Chief Superintendent paying courtesy calls on the legal establishment while a body grew colder all the time. But that was not to underestimate Roffey, whom he would not have assigned to the case unless he had had complete confidence in his abilities. It would be good for the morale of the C.I.D. to have a murder enquiry, especially if it could be brought to a quick and successful conclusion. The City's crime tended to be one track. Company fraud.

Meanwhile, back in his own office, Detective Chief Superintendent Roffey put his bowler back on, hooked his umbrella over his arm and leaned against the edge of his desk facing the door, waiting for Detective Sergeant Chisett.

The sight of Detective Chief Superintendent Roffey and Detective Sergeant Chisett together was apt to provoke a certain degree of secret amusement among their colleagues. Where Roffey was dapper and trim, Chisett was gangling and loose-limbed. The one, as already mentioned, was always impeccably dressed: the other's clothes managed to look as though they had been borrowed from a number of different people of varying shape and size. On this occasion he appeared in Roffey's room wearing a three-piece brown suit, each of whose pieces gave the impression of being a distant cousin of the other two. In one hand he clutched a well-worn raincoat and a brown felt hat with an extra wide brim which was, perhaps, his real hallmark. It was a hat which could be identified at a considerable distance, particularly on the head of its tall, loping owner. He was usually taken for some amiable visitor from the outback when seen in the vicinity of one of London's sights.

'Is the car there?' Roffey enquired, gazing at his sergeant without a tremor. As far as he was concerned it was up to people to dress as they wished and he knew that Sergeant Chisett's unpolicemanlike appearance hid a shrewd and lively mind combined with a special talent for never getting in a flap.

'Yes, sir.'

'You've heard what's happened?'

'Some barrister's been murdered in the Temple.'

Roffey nodded. 'Let's get along there then.'

On the way, Chisett said in a thoughtful voice, 'I could think of a fair number of candidates for sudden death in that place, but most of them judges. I gather this chappie was only a pupil.'

'Where'd you learn that?'

'D.C. Brown was recently in a case in which Mr Geddy was defending and he says this murdered chappie was his pupil. Name of Apple something or other.'

43

'Appleman.'

'Could be.'

'It is.'

The car, which had been crawling along the Embankment in the morning traffic jam while Chief Superintendent Roffey gazed sternly out of the window, now managed to extricate itself and reach the turn-in to the Temple.

Half-way up Middle Temple Lane, Roffey told the driver to stop and Chisett and he got out.

'Park the car as close as you can to Mulberry Court,' Roffey said. 'If you have any trouble, say that I'll fix it with the Benchers.' The driver nodded. He didn't even know what Benchers were and cared less. He would park the car where he wanted and soon see off anyone who tried to prevent him.

Roffey glanced about him as they made the last lap of their journey on foot. He secretly hoped that he might spot some senior barrister, or better still a judge, whom he knew and with whom he could exchange a respectful greeting. But the opportunity never came.

Nevertheless, their arrival in Mulberry Court itself went some way to satisfying his not inconsiderable sense of occasion. Instinct had prepared him so that even as they emerged into the small court and a number of idling press photographers had sprung into action, he had managed to pull a couple of paces ahead of Sergeant Chisett and to have set his features in an expression of determination, dignity and confidence. It was a historic fact that he had never been caught off balance by a photographer. It was rumoured that even royalty had wondered how it was done.

A constable, wearing the distinctive type of helmet seen on the heads of City policemen, was standing at the entrance to 4 Mulberry Court. He saluted as Roffey and Chisett passed inside. Another officer was stationed outside the actual door of Martin Ainsworth's Chambers. He also saluted, but fumblingly and only because he had seen his colleague at the main entrance do so.

A number of people were standing about in the small

lobby outside the clerks' room and Ainsworth detached himself as the two C.I.D. officers came through the door.

'Ah, Mr Roffey,' he said, 'I thought I'd stay until you came and I can, if necessary, hang on here for as long as you may want me. My clerk has made tentative arrangements to keep me free for the day. There's probably not much I can do, but, as head of Chambers, I am at your disposal.'

'Thank you, Mr Ainsworth, I should certainly wish to have a talk with you after I've viewed the scene and got things under way,' Roffey said importantly.

'Anything you say.'

With Ainsworth leading the way and Donald bringing up the rear, they set off down the passage to James Geddy's room. Ainsworth opened the door and stood aside.

'Nothing's been touched since the body was found just before nine o'clock this morning.'

'Who found it?'

'I did.' Donald's voice was a croak.

Roffey and Chisett entered the room and then stood staring in silence for a full minute at the grisly scene which met their eyes.

Robin sat sprawled in James Geddy's swivel chair like some helpless drunk. His head lolled over on his left shoulder and there was a terrible gash in his neck on the right side. The whole of his front was covered in dried blood and there was blood, too, on the desk and on the floor in the area of the chair.

'The weapon's on the floor beside his feet,' Ainsworth said, pointing in the direction.

Roffey moved a couple of paces and looked; then glanced enquiringly at Ainsworth.

'It's Mr Geddy's paperknife. He kept it on his desk.'

Roffey's gaze returned to the desk. Apart from the silver inkwell and the jade paperweight, there was only just a slim set of papers tied with pink tape over on one corner of the desk out of range of the bloodstains.

It was Martin Ainsworth who spoke again. 'Those are

the papers which kept Appleman hanging on in Chambers last night. They're connected with Mr Geddy's present case at the Old Bailey. Appleman was to wait for them and drop them at Mr Geddy's house on his own way home.'

'Who left them here?'

'I can't tell you. Someone from Finster, Slatter, the solicitors, I imagine.'

Roffey stared at them hard for a moment.

'What do they contain?'

'I can't tell you that either, I'm afraid. As I said, we haven't touched anything in this room and that includes everything on the desk.'

'Who was the last person to leave Chambers last night?' Roffey asked.

Ainsworth glanced at Donald, who swallowed as though he had something stuck in his throat and said, 'Sheila. She's the Chambers' typist.'

'I'd like to have a word with her.'

'She's not here,' Donald said uncomfortably. 'She came in, but we had to send her home. She was overcome by Mr Appleman's death. She broke down completely.'

Roffey raised an enquiring eyebrow, but Donald said no more and appeared to have become suddenly interested in the print which hung on the wall behind Geddy's desk.

'Where does she live?'

'Uh?'

'This girl, the typist. Where does she live?'

'Putney.'

'Why should she have been so upset by Mr Appleman's death?'

Donald shook his head vaguely. 'It could have happened over anyone.'

Roffey shot him a hard look which caused Donald to shift uneasily.

There was a brief and studied silence and then Martin Ainsworth spoke.

'I don't think there's any mystery or secret about it,' he said in a tone of calm authority, 'but Appleman was supposed to be rather fond of Sheila. That's so, isn't it, Donald?'

'Yes, sir, there was some sort of Chambers gossip to that effect.'

Roffey glanced from one to the other, but kept his thoughts to himself. It had, however, occurred to him of a sudden that he was witnessing the closing of professional ranks. He didn't believe they would go so far as to hide a murderer, but they would be quite capable of trying to throw him off the scent in order to cover up anything which might threaten their corporate respectability.

There was a sudden exclamation from Detective Sergeant Chisett, followed by a lunge across the room towards the window.

'Shoo!'

As the others turned in the same direction, they were in time to see part of a man rapidly disappearing from view.

'One of those bloody photographers,' Sergeant Chisett explained.

'Better go outside and remind them they're on private property and they'll find themselves in the Tower if they start taking liberties in these precincts,' Roffey said. 'And, at the same time, phone up for one of *our* photographers and ask Detective Sergeant Scott of the Fingerprint Branch to come along. Also ask for arrangements to be made for a pathologist to attend the scene. Professor Drayton, if possible.'

Chisett nodded. 'Which phone can I use?' he asked Donald.

'The one in the clerks' room. I'll come with you.'

Donald sounded relieved to have an excuse to depart. After they had gone, Roffey said casually, 'How long has he been your clerk, Mr Ainsworth?'

'Donald? He's been with us about twelve years now. Came when he was only eighteen. He's been the number one clerk for the past four years.'

'I've not come across him before, I don't think.'

'He's very good. One of the best of the new generation of

Temple clerks.'

Roffey smiled thinly. 'You have complete confidence in him, in fact?'

'Complete. We all have.'

'A great asset, a good clerk, I imagine,' Roffey observed, gazing thoughtfully around the room.

Ainsworth let the comment go. It didn't seem the moment to embark on a discussion of the merits of Donald in particular or of barristers' clerks in general. He made a move as though to leave the gruesome scene when Roffey's attention became focussed on the print behind the desk.

'They're pleasant those old prints of the Temple,' Roffey remarked. 'What is it, seventeenth century?'

'Yes, about mid-seventeenth,' Ainsworth replied tersely. 'Though this hardly seems the time to have a discussion about art.'

Roffey glanced at him with a faintly surprised expression. He had never intended entering on a discourse about art. On the other hand, he always tried to behave in a civilised fashion when he was in the company of someone whom he regarded as an equal in a kindred field. It was a question of observing the niceties of professional life. However, Martin Ainsworth Q.C. had fallen short of his expectations.

'Perhaps we can go to another room and you can tell me all you know about the dead young man,' he said, after the merest pause.

At that moment, there were sounds of heavy footsteps outside the door which was flung open to reveal the person of the Under-Treasurer of the Inn. Lieutenant-Colonel Forster was a retired cavalry officer whose position as Under-Treasurer combined the duties of bursar, steward and glorified clerk of the works.

He stopped short in the doorway as he caught sight of the body. Slowly he shook his head.

'He can't have known much after the first second of searing pain.' He looked up at Ainsworth. 'Bad business! Not good at all! Must do what we can to minimise the scandal aspect!'

'What scandal?' Roffey asked quickly and with a faint note of hope.

'Yes, I'm not clear what you mean by scandal,' Ainsworth said in a frosty voice.

'I mean the scandal of a barrister murdered in the Temple. In his Chambers. In this particular Inn. It's the sort of thing which could give rise to rumours of unimaginable proportions. The newspapers will thrive on hints of scandal in the profession. We must do everything we can to check it.'

Ainsworth, who happened to be a member of Gray's Inn and who therefore owed no special allegience to either the Inner or Middle Temple which between them owned all the property comprising the Temple, said in the same frosty tone, 'They'd better watch out before they start hinting at scandals in my Chambers. The unfortunate murder of a pupil doesn't turn 4 Mulberry Court into a hotbed of depravity and corruption.'

' 'Course it doesn't. But the sooner an arrest is made, the better for all of us.' He glanced from Ainsworth to Roffey. 'Have there been any suggestions as to who might have done it?'

Roffey shook his head. 'But I hope it won't be long, Colonel, before I've made some solid progress and can report success to your Benchers. I can assure you, of course, that we in the City Police shan't do anything to exacerbate the embarrassing position in which you gentlemen find yourselves.'

'The one emotion from which I am not suffering,' Ainsworth said spiritedly, 'is embarrassment. I'm stunned and shattered, but not embarrassed.'

'Quite,' the Under-Treasurer said with an emphatic nod. 'Terrible thing to have happened. You know that you can depend on everyone's co-operation, Superintendent.' He paused. 'I'm afraid I didn't actually catch your name.'

'Roffey. Detective *Chief* Superintendent Roffey.'

'Yes, of course. Well, I'd best be getting back. I'll read the Riot Act to those newspaper blighters on my way out.

Remind them they're on private property and had better watch their behaviour if they don't want to be slung out.'

'Leave them to me if you like, Colonel Forster,' Roffey said. 'I can handle them all right. Don't want to upset them unnecessarily. They're often quite a help on cases to us police. Even if not nearly as often as they like to think.'

'As you wish. Don't want to interfere. Keep me in touch with developments, Chief Superintendent.' He glanced back at Martin Ainsworth. 'Let me know if there's anything the Inn can do.'

'Thanks. I will.'

When the Under-Treasurer had gone, Roffey said, 'I'd like to talk to your clerk. Is there somewhere I can see him?'

'You can use my room.'

'Excellent. In due course, I shall need to interview all the members of Chambers.'

'They're all out in Court at the moment, but they'll be returning to Chambers in the course of the afternoon. If you want to see Mr Geddy, you can get hold of him at the Old Bailey during the luncheon adjournment.'

'Just what I had in mind. Perhaps someone can prepare a list for me of all the members of your Chambers.'

'Donald or Stephen can do that. Stephen's the number two clerk.'

'That would certainly be helpful. And you, Mr Ainsworth, you don't mind hanging on here a bit?'

'No. I'll stay as long as you require me.'

'That's most co-operative of you,' Roffey said in his smoother tone.

There was no doubt that Donald, a normally resilient, even perky, person, who could hold his own endlessly with rebellious barristers and carping solicitors, was distinctly nervous and ill at ease when confronted alone by Detective Chief Superintendent Roffey.

Roffey gazed at him dispassionately. He had no reason to suspect him of anything at the moment. On the other hand, everyone in Chambers was a suspect in one sense. They formed the small community from which a victim had been claimed. Inevitably, suspicion must hover over them.

'I'd like you to take me through the sequence of events of yesterday evening,' Roffey said in his quiet measured tone. 'I gather that Mr Appleman had agreed to wait in Chambers until some papers in Mr Geddy's case were delivered?'

'Yes.'

'Now what time did you yourself leave?'

'About half past six.'

'And who was still here when you departed?'

'Just Mr Appleman and Sheila.'

'No one else at all?'

'No.'

'I see! Who had been the last to leave immediately before *you*?'

'Mr Quant and his pupil, Mr March.'

'How long before?'

'Ten or fifteen minutes.'

'What about Mr Geddy, when did he leave?'

'He went straight home from the Bailey.'

'And Stephen, your assistant?'

'He left about six o'clock. Probably a bit earlier.'

'Who has keys to Chambers?'

'Everyone. At least, not the pupils.'

'But all the barristers?'

'Yes, plus Stephen and Sheila and myself.'

'That the lot?'

'Oh, the cleaner, Mrs Piper. She has a key.'

'When does she come in?'

'Normally about seven o'clock in the evening. But she didn't come last night. Her daughter phoned up to say she was ill.'

'When did the daughter phone?'

'In the morning.'

'I see.' Roffey stared over the top of Donald's head with a judicial air. Donald licked his lips and focused his own stare on his inquisitor's chin. It was a firm, smoothly shaven and somewhat intimidating chin. Roffey lowered his gaze till his eyes rested on Donald's worried face. 'Coming now to the events of this morning. What time did you arrive?'

'About a quarter past nine.'

'Is that your usual time?'

'I come in any time between just after nine and just after half past.'

'And you were the first person in?'

'Yes.'

'Though with so many keys in existence, anyone could have come in and gone out again without your knowledge?'

'Yes.'

'Hmm. And what did you do when you first came in?'

'Went into the clerks' room. I wanted to see whether Sheila had completed the typing she stayed on to do.'

'And had she?'

Donald gulped and shook his head. 'No.'

'Had she nearly completed it?'

'No, it didn't look as though she had been able to get very far.'

'Did that surprise you?'

'Well, I suppose it did. Though I'm sure she had a good reason.'

Roffey gave a small, wintry smile. 'There are always reasons for everything. Sometimes good, sometimes bad. Doubtless we shall find out which Sheila's were. And having discovered that the typing she'd stayed to do wasn't finished, what did you do next?'

'I went along to Mr Geddy's room.'

Roffey raised an eyebrow. 'Oh, why was that?'

'To see whether these papers had come.'

'But I thought Mr Appleman was to deliver them at Mr Geddy's home last night?'

'That's right.'

'Then I don't quite follow what you'd find by looking in his room?'

'I wanted to make sure that Mr Appleman had waited and that the papers weren't sitting on Mr Geddy's desk.'

'Oh, I see! And it was then you discovered the crime?'

'Yes. I didn't touch anything, I went straight to the phone.'

'And called the police?'

'I phoned Mr Ainsworth at his home first, then the police.'

'Who else in Chambers did you phone?'

'I tried to get Mr Geddy, but he'd left home.'

'Have you spoken to him since?'

'No, but I sent Stephen to the Bailey to tell him what had happened.'

'I see!'

'Well, I had to let him know why he hadn't received the further papers he was expecting from Finster, Slatter.'

Roffey brushed aside the explanation.

'What time did Sheila arrive?'

'About a quarter to ten. That's her usual time.'

'And you told her what had happened, I suppose?'

'Yes. And she ... she went all to pieces. She just broke down.'

'Did she go along to Mr Geddy's room?'

'Good heavens no!' Donald's voice was shocked.

'Did you ask her why she hadn't finished her typing?'

'No. I didn't ask her anything. She was too upset.'

'So you didn't even find out whether those papers on Mr Geddy's desk had been delivered before she went home last night or not? Or whether Mr Appleman was still here when she left?'

Donald shook his head.

'A pity!' Roffey's tone held a note of distinct reproach. 'However, we can doubtless find out later, though it would have been helpful to have had her immediate answers to those important questions.'

Donald coloured. 'If you'd seen her, Mr Roffey, you wouldn't have felt like asking her questions. Apart from which, you wouldn't have got any straight answers. Sensible answers, I mean,' he added quickly.

'Just tell me how you broke the news to her.'

'Well as soon as she came she could see that something

was up with me and I told her straight away that something awful had happened. I said that Mr Appleman was dead in Mr Geddy's room. That he'd been killed.'

'And she broke down?'

'Yes, she went very white and swayed so that I thought she was going to faint. Then she just collapsed into a chair and cried and cried.'

'Did she say anything at all?'

'No, she only gasped when I told her he was dead.'

'She didn't exclaim anything?'

'No, definitely not.'

'Now, what about this "Chambers gossip" I think you called it, that Mr Appleman was rather fond of Sheila. What's the truth of that?'

Donald squirmed on his chair.

'There's really nothing to tell about it. He used to hang around her a bit and that's about all. We treated it as something of a joke. It wasn't serious or anything like that.'

'And what was her reaction?'

'She treated it as a joke as well. She has a boy-friend to whom she's semi-engaged. I know she didn't have any special feelings towards Mr Appleman.'

'I see!' Roffey said. He had a disturbing way of uttering the phrase so as to make it sound heavy with meaning.

For several seconds, he gazed thoughtfully at his bowler hat, which he had carefully laid on the side of Ainsworth's desk after blowing away some specks of dust.

Donald observed him with a now utterly resigned expression. He still found it difficult to realise what had happened, though slowly the feeling of numbed shock was beginning to lift. He wished he could get away and be alone for a short time. Obviously the police had to be given every reasonable assistance, but his first allegiance was still to Chambers and its members.

There was a knock on the door and Detective Sergeant Chisett's head appeared round the edge.

'Sergeant Scott's here, sir, and Professor Drayton's on his way. And I've told the press that if they're good boys, you'll tell them what you can later in the day.' He looked across at Donald with a faintly amused expression. 'And your girl, Sheila, has just come in. Yeh, I thought that might surprise you!'

IV

James Geddy was feeling distinctly tetchy when he arrived at the Old Bailey that morning. His pupil had failed to drop the papers he needed at his home the previous evening and, knowing Robin, he was unlikely to arrive until the fifty-ninth minute of the eleventh hour. This would inevitably mean hoarse whispers with Slatter in Court which was quite the least satisfactory form of communication lawyers had recourse to. And worse than that when the other person had apparently feasted off garlic the night before which, in Geddy's experience, was all too often the case!

He had intended to call in at Chambers on his way to the Old Bailey and see if the errant papers were there, but then he had got badly held up in traffic and had decided to drive direct to Court and phone Stephen to come and pick up his car from whatever illegal place he had managed to park it. To make him crosser, the traffic had suddenly melted so that he would after all have had time to call in at the Temple. He was just about to leave the robing-room to go and telephone Chambers when David March appeared.

'Oh, hello,' Geddy said in a not particularly friendly tone, 'what are you doing at the Bailey?' Before David could answer, he added, 'You haven't seen Robin this morning, have you?'

David shook his head. 'No. Actually, I wondered whether I could attach myself to you to-day. Philip's gone down to Dover on a plea and he said it wasn't worth while my trekking there, too.'

'By all means come and hold my hand.' He frowned. 'I

55

wish to hell I knew what had happened to Robin and those papers he was meant to be bringing me.'

David looked uncomfortable. 'Shall I go and phone Chambers?'

'I was just about to go and do that myself. But hold on! Here's Stephen...'

'Oh, Mr Geddy, Donald sent me to tell you. Something terrible's happened. Mr Appleman's dead. Someone's killed him.'

'You can't mean it!'

'He's been ... been stabbed ... murdered.'

Geddy shook his head in disbelief while David just stared at Stephen, mouth open and face the colour of his own clean white collar.

James Geddy's voice trembled when he spoke next. 'Where did this happen?'

'In Chambers, sir. In your room. They found him dead in your chair this morning. Donald did when he arrived.'

'I can't believe it! I simply can't believe it!'

'It's true!'

'Yes, of course, it's true, but...' He put a hand up to his forehead and pressed his temples. It was over a minute before he spoke again. 'Does anyone know what happened?'

'No. The police were arriving just as I left. Mr Ainsworth's there.'

There was another silence. Then Geddy said almost sharply, 'I must go and phone Chambers immediately. Wait for me outside Court, David.'

While David March and Stephen made their way down to the Court, Stephen gave David a fuller, if still somewhat incoherent, account of the discovery of Robin's body.

'But who on earth could have murdered him?' David burst out.

Stephen gave him a wild, sidelong glance.

'All I know is that *I* didn't.'

'Good lord, I hope that goes for everyone in Chambers!'

'Well, someone did and made a proper job of it, too.'

'It must have been a burglar.'

This time Stephen's look was pitying. 'There's no evidence of a burglary and it doesn't make sense anyway.'

'O.K., then, who do you think did it?'

Stephen started at the directness of the question. Then his face went blank and he shook his head. 'There are times when it's not healthy to speculate.'

It seemed to David that Stephen's manner was odd to say the least. He was usually uninhibitedly chatty and forthcoming. But now he was playing the role of the possessor of dark secrets. With a mental shrug, David asked, 'Who's the officer in charge of the case?'

Stephen's expression changed as a grin broke over his face. ' "Fancy spats"!'

'Who the hell is "fancy spats"?'

'Detective Chief Superintendent Roffey of the City Police. Haven't you met him?'

David shook his head. 'Wouldn't this be a case for the Yard murder squad?'

'Not unless the City people ask for their help. Anyway, "fancy spats" is a pretty efficient officer. It's just the thought of him caught up in a bit of mess and blood that's funny. He looks like the chairman of a ruddy bank dressed to meet the stockholders.'

'And he really wears spats?'

'Actually he doesn't wear them at all, but you sort of feel he should.'

'Well, I hope he arrests Robin's murderer in double quick time,' David said, glancing past Stephen. 'Ah, here's Mr Geddy.'

James Geddy's expression was grave and troubled as he rejoined them.

'I've spoken to Donald and also had a word with Martin. It's suggested that I carry on with the Manion case this morning and make myself available to the police during the lunch adjournment. I gather I'm not required back in Chambers immediately. They've got enough to be going on with.' He looked at David. 'Did you ever meet Robin's parents?'

'No. I don't think anyone has. No one in Chambers, I mean. They never came up to London. He's only been home for a weekend once since he became your pupil.'

'But he got on all right with them so far as you know?'

'Yes.'

'I only ask because I shall have to get in touch with them myself and it would have helped to know something about them.' He looked at his watch. 'I must go round and see the judge and tell him what's happened. Perhaps one of you would let Peter Strange know. And someone had better find Adrian Slatter and explain things to him. Though I don't imagine this is the sort of news that'll take long to spread through the building.' He groaned. 'What a morning to have to take Manion along the evidential tightrope on which he's set his nimble feet!' He shook his head despairingly.

He had just left them to go and see the judge when Holly Childersley came dashing up. She looked close to tears.

'David, what's this awful news about Robin?'

'I'm afraid it's true. He was murdered in Chambers last night. Donald found him in James' room this morning.'

Holly blinked her eyes as the tears began to overflow.

'But who could have done such a terrible thing? Poor Robin! I just can't believe it.'

David put out an awkward hand to comfort her. He was fond of Holly, but the fact that they were both robed was somehow inhibiting. The more so as, at the best of times, her wig gave the impression of being so precariously perched that a faint breeze would be sufficient to dislodge it. He gingerly patted her shoulder.

'Let's meet during the adjournment. What Court are you in?'

'Anthea's prosecuting before Grigg. It's a fight and'll last all day.'

'O.K., we'll meet then. Either in Court 1 or in Grigg's Court. Whichever of us gets out first can come to the other. Now, I must fly, Holly, I have to find Adrian Slatter and explain things to him before the Court sits.' He gave her arm a cautious squeeze. 'Bear up,' he said with a small conspiratorial smile, 'if the police can't discover who killed poor old Robin, you and I will.'

Holly's obvious distress touched a chord in his own emotions. He recalled his short but sharp display of irritation with Robin the previous evening in Chambers when he had flung that remark at him about having a chip on his shoulder, accompanied by the snide comment about hanging around Sheila. Tears pricked his eyes as he recalled that they were the last words he spoke to Robin. How wretched and damnable life could be! Didn't the Bible have something about never letting the sun go down on one's wrath? Well, in his case it was not wrath so much as pique on which the sun had set. He had, at least, stood up for Robin afterwards when Philip Quant had spoken of him in abrasive terms, but Robin would never know that. He felt rotten and miserable to a degree he had seldom experienced.

It was while he was standing there unable to break out of the pall of gloom which had suddenly descended over him that Adrian Slatter came dashing up. One glance at his face was enough to show that he had already heard the news. He looked stunned and shocked, almost haggard.

'Is it true about Robin Appleman?' he asked. 'I heard when I came into the building just now.'

'I'm afraid it is.'

'I can hardly believe it.'

'None of us can.'

'Do they know who . . .'

David shook his head. 'James Geddy's gone to see the judge,' he said, 'he asked me to tell you.'

'Is the trial going to be adjourned?'

'I don't think so.' He gave the solicitor a wan smile. 'There's no real reason why it should be.'

'I thought maybe the police would want to interview Mr Geddy this morning.'

'I don't think there's much he can tell them. He never went back to Chambers last night.'

'Of course not, I remember now.' His hand flew up to his

mouth. 'Oh my God! Those papers I sent round . . .' David stared at him, waiting for him to go on. It was several seconds before he did so. 'What time was he murdered?'

'I don't know. Only that he was found dead this morning.'

'He was going to wait in Chambers for some papers in the Manion case I was to try and lay my hands on and send round for Mr Geddy.'

'I know. What time did you send them?'

'It must have been about seven o'clock. My chief clerk, George Uppard, took them.' He paused. 'I haven't seen him this morning. He was going straight to South London Court.'

'It looks as though he may be an important witness,' David said.

Slatter nodded slowly. 'It certainly does. I wonder whom he handed the papers to?'

'Probably to Sheila if she was still around. Otherwise to Robin himself.'

Slatter brooded for a time.

'I wonder what's happened to the papers,' he said at last, apparently thinking aloud rather than addressing David.

'What were they, anyway?' David asked after a further silence between them.

'I beg your pardon?'

'These papers you sent round to Chambers, are they vital to the case?'

'I don't think so, but it's really for Mr Geddy to say.'

Slatter's voice seemed to come from far away, which was certainly where his thoughts were. He shook himself. 'I'm so sorry, I'm afraid my mind was elsewhere.'

David had no doubt where it was either – trying to assess the implications of his clerk's visit to Chambers the previous evening.

Slatter went on, 'It's a bundle of correspondence, about ten letters in all between Manion and one of the prosecution's witnesses. As I say, I don't think it particularly assists the defence, but Mr Geddy may feel otherwise. If

I'd thought it important, I'd have included them in the brief in the first place. As it was, I had the hell of a job finding them. I've had a series of temporary secretaries recently, so that nothing's filed where you might expect. And I'm not the tidiest of people in the first place. On top of which Manion has bombarded me with enough documents to paper every court in this building.' He looked at his watch. 'It's nearly twenty past ten, I must go and see Manion before the Court sits. Will you tell Mr Geddy where I am?' He ran a hand through his hair and then patted it back into place.

After he had gone, David made his way into Court and sat down. He stared fixedly at the desk ledge in front of him in the hope that no one would come up and talk. He wanted to think. If Robin had not been murdered by a casual intruder, the implications were almost too grim to contemplate. Why Robin? What harm had he done anyone? He had worked harder than most to get to the Bar, only to be snuffed out as though his hopes and ambitions, his joys and his disappointments mattered nothing. The one thing he was sure of, it couldn't possibly be anyone in Chambers. Barristers might have all manner of failings, but they didn't go about murdering one another. They were a civilised breed whose weapons were forensic rather than lethal. Anyway, everyone in Chambers liked Robin. Well, almost everyone ... he wondered what it could be that his own pupil-master, Philip Quant had against him. That had come as a shock, but it certainly couldn't have anything to do with Robin's death. In any event, Philip and he had left Chambers together and gone up to the Templar where they had spent half an hour or so drinking. Admittedly they had parted company outside the public house, but Philip had made for a bus stop while he, David, had walked back through the Temple to take the Underground.

He gave a small shiver. He prayed that answer to the questions now swirling through his head might soon be found and Robin's murderer quickly identified. If not, he could foresee a period of increasing tension in

Chambers until life became unbearable.

Without lifting his head, he glanced about him covertly. The Court was beginning to fill. People were gathered in small whispering huddles. Even with his eyes shut, he felt he would have known something untoward had happened.

'I've had a word with the judge. He's going to make a brief announcement and then the trial goes on.' James Geddy had slipped into his seat almost before David was aware of his presence. 'I've told him,' Geddy went on, 'that I've not yet seen the document Manion referred to in his evidence yesterday so that I can't assess its relevance.'

'I gather from Slatter that it's correspondence between Manion and a prosecution witness. He didn't seem to think it was very material.'

'Oh, it's letters, is it! Where is Slatter?'

'With Manion.'

At that moment, Peter Strange entered Court and came straight across to Geddy.

'I'm appalled by this news, James ... A shocking thing to have happened ... If there's anything I can do ...'

'Thanks, Peter, I'll let you know. Meanwhile it seems best to soldier on.'

'I'm very sorry to hear about this tragedy, Mr Geddy.' This time the speaker was Detective Chief Superintendent Peters who had come over to where James Geddy sat.

David found it almost a relief when three knocks on the door heralded the judge's entry, at the same time Adrian Slatter came scurrying up from the cells.

Mr Justice Tyler glanced round the courtroom as though to make sure everyone was present. He gave a small nod to the prison officer who was standing at the top of the dock steps waiting for the sign to put Manion up. He moved to one side on receipt of the nod and Frank Manion appeared, moving with customary briskness to the front of the dock where he made his own careful survey of those present. The judge motioned him to sit down and he did so after a pause sufficient to demonstrate that he was doing so of his own and no one else's volition.

David watched him throughout this small but perfectly controlled performance. The man certainly radiated something, he thought. Something about as welcome as an anaconda's approach. He could understand why Robin had felt sorry for Adrian Slatter. On the other hand Slatter must by now be well used to coping with clients of this type. His whole practice was built on them. And a highly lucrative practice, too, by every account!

Slatter turned round to whisper something to James Geddy, who motioned him into silence as the judge began to speak.

'The Court has this morning learnt with regret of the tragic and untimely death of Mr Robin Appleman, a young member of the Bar and pupil of Mr Geddy. Pupillage is a vital training period for newly called barristers and it was in this Court that Mr Appleman was giving his diligent attendance until he met his death some time in the night. It is neither right nor desirable that I should say more at this moment, but, equally, the occasion required that we should stand in silence for half a minute as a mark of respect for one who was so recently among us and whom death has claimed with such suddenness.'

Mr Justice Tyler stood and, on cue, everyone else rose to their feet to an accompaniment of scraping chairs and dropped articles.

David glanced towards Manion who was staring straight at the judge with a bored, faintly contemptuous expression. Mr Justice Tyler himself stood with hands clasped in front of him and head bowed. James Geddy had adopted a similar pose, as had Adrian Slatter, save that his head was bowed so low that his chin appeared to be sunk right on to his chest. David felt a faint tinge of guilt when his own wandering gaze met that of Chief Superintendent Peters, who was taking the opportunity of covertly observing the expressions of others. David hoped his feeling of guilt had not shown itself; or, if it had, that it would not be misconstrued.

The judge sat down and his clerk, who was standing behind him, pushed the huge throne-like chair forward a few inches. It ran on rollers and David had the sudden piquant mindseye picture of the chair sliding forward out of control and squashing Her Majesty's judge against his desk.

'You were examining your client, Mr Geddy, when we adjourned yesterday. Let him return to the witness box.' Mr Justice Tyler watched Manion make his way from the dock and when he reached the witness-box, said, 'You're still under oath, remember!'

Manion responded with a curt nod and it struck David what an anachronism the oath was for witnesses like him, to whom truth was only relevant if it was expedient. No form of words could bind the conscience of a Manion, simply because the Manions of this world didn't possess that mysterious and often troublesome piece of mechanism. On the other hand the oath was tied to a sanction which bit if you told lies in the witness-box. Or rather if anyone could prove you had told lies, which was a very different thing in practice, as even a novice lawyer like David was aware.

James Geddy turned towards the judge. 'You will recall, my lord, that my client referred in his evidence yesterday to a document which would prove a point he was making. My lord, I am in some difficulty as the document in question – I undersand that, in fact, it is a bundle of correspondence – was delivered at my Chambers last night by my instructing solicitor. However, for reasons which I need not perhaps expand on, it is not available to me at this moment, though I hope I may have these further papers before my client concludes his evidence. In those circumstances, I shall be grateful if your lordship will permit me to move on from that particular aspect of Mr Manion's evidence and return to it later.'

'Certainly, Mr Geddy.'

'I am much obliged, my lord.'

And so, on the surface at least, the calm, unhurried pattern of an English criminal trial reasserted itself and imposed its discipline on all its participants.

Nevertheless, David was not the only person in Court to

find his mind insistently straying to the whys and where-
fores of Robin's death. But being in Court was like being
held incommunicado and he found himself longing for the
end of the morning and the release which it would bring.

Newspapermen, on the other hand, were in and out all
the time and it was obvious that Manion's trial was no
longer their prime interest. Adrian Slatter also ducked out
two or three times to make phone calls, giving David a
fleeting, wan smile as he tiptoed past him on each occasion.

David noticed that Manion's eyes followed his solicitor's
every movement, though his concentration never seemed to
falter and James Geddy never had to repeat a question.

It was less than an hour since David had first learnt of
Robin's death, but already he felt he had lived with the
grim reality for much longer. Already his perspective was
in danger of becoming distorted by the capricious insinua-
tion of suspicion.

V

Sheila looked at Detective Chief Superintendent Roffey
with intense dislike. She was glad that she found it so easy
to dislike him, as it gave her strength and resolution in the
interview which had just begun. She was affronted by his
calm, aloof air of self-assurance, by the formal politeness
which seemed to patronise her and by his over-well-dressed
appearance which showed him, in her eyes, to be vain and
prissy. But secretly she found the overall impression intimidating, though this was something she was unwilling to
admit even to herself.

They were seated in Martin Ainsworth's room. A room
in which she normally felt comfortably at home, but which
had suddenly assumed the sinister air of one at K.G.B.
headquarters.

For several seconds Roffey had been staring at her in

silence. A procedure which, she was sure, was designed to unnerve her. But whatever she might be feeling inside, she met his gaze with an expression of resigned patience.

He made a sudden, small fastidious movement with one of his well-manicured hands and said, 'Well now, Miss Hamer, I'd like you to tell me in your own words about yesterday evening. I've established that when Donald left at half past six you and the deceased were the only two persons remaining in Chambers. Will you now take it from there?'

'I left about half an hour after Donald,' Sheila said in a voice which she tried to make sound natural. 'I . . .'

'Why? Why did you leave then?' There was a silence while each stared at the other before Roffey went on, 'As I understood it, Miss Hamer, you stayed on to finish some typing, but, as I also understand it, you didn't complete your work. There was obviously a reason – doubtless a very good reason – for your leaving earlier than you'd intended. What was it?'

'I had rather a headache.'

'You often get them?' Roffey enquired languidly.

'Not often, but sometimes.'

'Very well. Now during this half-hour that you were in Chambers after Donald had gone, did anyone call?'

'On the telephone, do you mean?'

Roffey looked at her sharply. She seemed to have recovered remarkably quickly for one who only shortly before had had to go home in hysterics. Sheila, who diagnosed the look, realised that she must not allow her dislike of the man to trap her into trying to score off him.

'First, did anyone call on the telephone? Secondly, did anyone call in person?' Roffey said, a dangerous edge to his tone.

Sheila nodded as though she now understood just what he meant. Police officers did not like being given lip by those they were interviewing. And certainly not officers of Roffey's rank and personality. They were liable to react disagreeably.

'Mr Slatter, the solicitor, phoned to say that he would be sending round the papers for Mr Geddy within the next half hour. That was the only phone call. But I'd left before they came.'

Roffey appeared to contemplate this information as he might examine a fish for bones in order to decide which end he should begin eating.

'Did Mr Slatter say who would be delivering the papers?'

'He said that his clerk, George Uppard, would be bringing them round.'

'Did you tell Mr Appleman?'

'Yes. I went along to Mr Geddy's room and told him.'

'What was he doing?'

'I didn't really notice. I just stuck my head round the door, told him and left.'

'Where was he?'

'I've just told you, he was in Mr Geddy's room.'

'Yes, but where in Mr Geddy's room?'

'He was sitting at the desk.'

'In the same chair in which he was found dead?'

'I don't know which chair he was found dead in,' Sheila said in a wary tone.

'Mr Geddy's desk chair. Was that the one he was sitting in?'

'Yes.'

'And how long after this was it that you decided to go home?'

'About ten minutes.'

'Because of your headache?'

'Yes.'

'Had it been coming on for a long time?'

Sheila gave a small shrug of annoyance.

'Not particularly.'

'How long?'

'I'm afraid I don't know. I'm not in the habit of timing my headaches.'

I'm sure you're not, young lady, Roffey thought to himself, just as I'm equally sure that it was no headache that decided you to go home early last night.

'And when did you next see Mr Appleman?'

'I didn't.'

'Not at all?'

'No ... er, yes, of course I did. But only for a second when I went back to Mr Geddy's room to tell him I was going.'

'And where was he then?'

'Still sitting in the chair.'

'Doing?'

'Nothing as far as I can remember.'

'And what did you say to him on that occasion?'

'I told him I was going home.'

'Did you tell him about your headache?'

'I think I probably did.'

'It must have been very bad by that time?'

'It was.'

'So you probably would have mentioned it?'

'Yes.'

'I have the impression, Miss Hamer, that you regard my questions with considerable suspicion. Am I right?'

'No, of course not. But it's only natural that I should want to answer them carefully. After all, presumably you wouldn't be asking them if the answers weren't important.'

'Oh, your answers are certainly important. I just hope that they are also truthful.'

Sheila flinched as though he had slapped her face. Roffey observed the reaction with satisfaction. He had no sympathy with her. Witnesses who prevaricated and lied – especially witnesses from the lower end of any hierarchical ladder – completely forfeited his indulgence. Not that this was ever a very plentiful commodity in his particular interviewer's kit.

Sheila, for her part, felt her legs go suddenly weak. The strain of the interview was beginning to tell and she hoped it might be nearing its end. As it was, she was thankful that she was sitting down and that her knees, which had begun to tremble uncontrollably, were hidden from her tormentor by the desk.

'Can we go on?' Roffey asked.

'Of course.'

'Let me know if you wish to break off for any reason. A headache, for instance . . .'

'I'm ready to answer your questions. I take it I'm not required to reply to your comments,' Sheila said, giving him a look which might have turned other men to stone.

'And so you told Mr Appleman you were going home and you left?'

'Yes.'

'With your work unfinished?'

'Yes.'

'Apart from the two occasions you've mentioned when you went along to Mr Geddy's room, did you see Mr Applman at all between the time Donald left and your own departure?'

'No.'

'He never came to the clerks' room?'

'No.'

'Didn't that surprise you?'

'Why should it?'

'I understood that Mr Appleman rather enjoyed your company,' Roffey remarked in a velvety tone.

'Who told you that?' Sheila demanded sharply.

'It was no secret, was it?'

'I don't know what anyone's been telling you, but there was nothing whatsoever between Mr Appleman and myself.'

'Maybe not, but he could still have been attracted by you. Was he?'

It was several seconds before Sheila replied, during which time her gaze flitted wildly like a small caged bird.

'Yes, he seemed to be.'

'How did he show it?'

'By . . . by seeking my company.' And then in anticipation of the next question, she added quickly, 'But not last night.'

'How odd, Miss Hamer! I would have thought last night would have been a golden opportunity with just the two of you alone in Chambers.'

'I'm afraid I can't answer for Mr Appleman.'

'And, alas, he can't answer for himself! At all events, what you're saying is that he made no approaches to you last night?'

'That's right.'

'You stayed in the clerks' room and he remained in Mr Geddy's room?'

'Yes.'

'You must have been thankful for that in view of your bad headache?'

'I was glad,' she retorted firmly, 'not only on account of my headache.'

Roffey affected to ignore her tone and said, 'When you departed, did you lock the door behind you?'

'No, I left the catch up, so that the person bringing the papers from Slatter's could get in.'

'I seem to remember the door says "knock and enter"?'

'Yes, I think most Chambers have that on their outside doors.'

'So Slatter's man would have knocked and entered and waited for Mr Appleman to appear?'

'I suppose so.'

'Hmm! And what time did you actually leave Chambers?'

'Near enough seven o'clock.'

'Can you remember whether it was before or after seven?'

'I think it was probably just after.'

'Why do you think that?'

'Because I don't remember hearing any of the clocks in the area striking the hour as I left.'

'You think you would have remembered that?'

'Yes.'

'Even with a headache?'

'Even more so with a headache,' Sheila said, almost viciously.

'Did you go straight home?'

'More or less.'

'What does that mean?'

'My boy-friend drove me home.'

'Oh!' Roffey managed to invest the exclamation with a wealth of implied meaning. 'What's his name?'

'Alan Dixon.'

'Did he pick you up from Chambers?'

'No.'

'Where did you meet, then?'

'We met at a pub just off the Strand. It's near his office. We often meet there in the evening and he drives me home.'

'A sort of standing arrangement you mean?'

'Yes.'

'Where does he live?'

'Wimbledon. With his parents.'

'And you live at Putney, I believe?'

'Yes. With mine.'

'Can you give me an address or telephone number where I can get hold of Mr Dixon?'

'Yes. Do you want it now?'

'No, later will do. How long did you stay in the pub with Mr Dixon?'

'Not long because I told him I had a headache and wanted to go home. I just had a tonic water while he finished his beer.'

'What time did you arrive at your home in Putney?'

'It must have been about eight-fifteen or eight-thirty. I remember it took longer than usual because we got stuck in a traffic jam by Putney Bridge.'

'Were your parents in when you got back?'

'No, they were out for the evening.'

'So there's no one who can confirm the exact time you arrived home?' Roffey said, in the same needling tone he had used so often during the interview.

'Alan can.'

'Yes, but apart from him?'

'No one.'

'And then this morning you arrived here about a quarter to ten?'

'Yes.'

'And...?'

'Donald told me the dreadful thing that had happened.'

'You were deeply affected by the news?'

'Of course I was. What would you have expected me to be?'

'Try and keep calm, Miss Hamer. I'm only seeking to elicit the sequence of events.'

'Donald saw how upset I was and suggested I ought to go home.'

'Which you did! But less than an hour later, you've recovered sufficiently to return ... Well, Miss Hamer?'

'I don't quite understand your tone! If you're hinting there's something in my conduct that calls for explanation, then perhaps you'd say so.'

Roffey studied her in silence for a full minute. When he spoke, his tone was uncompromising. 'Either you're being obtuse, Miss Hamer, which I don't believe, or you're trying to impede my enquiries. Yes, *impede*! You know quite well what I mean and I think it's time you made up your mind to co-operate with me, rather than behave like a difficult child. You should be better aware than most that a murder enquiry is not like a jolly quiz on T.V. and that it's everyone's public duty to assist the police in every way they can.'

Sheila, who had gone very white during this castigation, now appeared to be on the verge of tears. Her mouth trembled as she tried to speak and she had to pause for several seconds before going on.

'I don't know what I've done to deserve this,' she said tremulously, 'but ever since I came into this room, you've been bullying me, more or less calling me a liar and generally treating me like a criminal.' Her voice was becoming more spirited with each word she spoke. 'I don't know if this is the way you always treat witnesses, but if it is, I'm surprised if you ever solve any of your cases.'

'Shouting abuse at me is not going to help you, Miss Hamer! It merely prolongs things for both of us. Now, I'll give you one last chance to tell me why you returned to Chambers this morning so soon after you'd retired home in hysterics.' He seemed to read her expression for he went on, 'And if you're wondering what I'll do if you don't tell me, the answer is that I'll draw my own conclusions – and they're unlikely to be in your favour. So make up your mind which way it's to be.'

'There's nothing to tell,' Sheila said sullenly after a pause. 'I *did* feel better by the time I'd got home and I decided I ought to return to Chambers as I'd probably be wanted for interview' – she threw him a look of indignant reproach – 'and also because it was my duty to be here at such a time. I may be only the typist,' she added in a tone which might have landed her a part at the National Theatre, 'but I'm still regarded as one of Chambers.'

Roffey blinked, but otherwise appeared unmoved. 'So that's why you're back here,' he said aloud, but seemingly to himself. 'Does your boy-friend know of the murder?'

Sheila lifted her head slowly and met Roffey's gaze before she replied.

'Yes. I phoned him after I'd got home this morning.' Her voice held a note of challenge.

'Was it anything he said which decided you to come back to Chambers?'

'No. In fact, he suggested that I should spend the day at home.'

'Well, Miss Hamer, that seems to be about all for the time being,' Roffey said after a ruminative pause. 'I shall doubtless have further questions to ask you later on. Meanwhile, we must get down in statement form what you've told me. The important parts, anyway.'

He rose, walked round the desk and held the door open

for her. Sheila passed by him without a glance, to the surprised and faintly apprehensive notice of Martin Ainsworth and Donald who were standing talking outside the clerks' room. Sheila ignored them, too, and went straight to her typewriter which she began attacking with single-minded vigour.

'Everything go all right?' Donald enquired anxiously, following her into the room.

She ceased typing as suddenly as she had begun. 'I think he's the rudest, unkindest, most hateful man I've ever come across,' she said in an explosion of feeling and then immediately burst into tears.

Donald gazed at her with a mixture of dismay and irritation.

'Perhaps it'd be as well if you went home after all,' he said wearily.

'What! And have that man think I've run away from him!' she exclaimed through sobs. She made a vague waving motion in Donald's direction. 'I'm sorry, I'll be all right in a moment, I promise I will.'

Detective Sergeant Chisett, who had caught sight of the tail end of the scene as he came back into Chambers (he had been in and out the whole of the past hour), knocked on the door of Ainsworth's room and entered. He found Roffey sitting comfortably at the desk writing notes on the slim tear-off pad he always carried in his waistcoat pocket with the gold propelling pencil which was another item of his equipment.

'Girl seems to be having another attack of hysterics from the look and sound of her,' Chisett observed.

'Where is she?'

'In the clerks' room.'

'She tried to fence with me,' Roffey said coldly, 'and then became all soft and hurt when I put her in her place. I don't know whom she thought she was fooling in the first place.'

'Think she knows something about the murder, sir?'

But all Roffey said was, 'We must have a word with her

74

boy-friend before he and she have any further chance of putting their heads together.'

'So that's it, is it?'

'That's what it looks like.'

Chisett nodded his head in a knowing fashion. Then: 'The room's been done for fingerprints, including the papers on the desk.'

'Have you looked at those yet?'

'Yeah, I did it while Sergeant Scott was examining them for prints.'

'And?'

'Just letters between Manion and someone called Birtle about some money which had been lent to a third bloke called Pinky. Funny how often crooks seem to have nicknames more suited to woolly toys!'

'Who'd lent the money, Manion or Birtle?'

'It appeared that both of them had at one time or another.'

Roffey pursed his lips. 'I'd better glance through them and then if Scott has finished with them we can release them to Mr Geddy.' He looked at his watch. 'Where the devil's Professor Drayton? He should be here by now.'

'He is.' In the doorway, the pathologist fixed Roffey with a beady eye. 'If you'd keep the streets freer of traffic, I'd have been here much sooner. And as for trying to park a car in this legal holy of holies, it'd be easier to nick the Benchers' port. I mention all this merely to indicate that I'm in no mood for reproaches for being late.'

'I'm sorry you've had so much bother,' Roffey said in one of his rare moments of sounding abashed. 'Let me show you the body right away.'

VI

George Uppard knew all the people who mattered at London's various Magistrates' Courts. That is to say, he knew the jailers, the warrant officers and, though less important in his view, the Court inspectors. He also knew most of the regular crime reporters, probation officers and ushers, as well as at least one official in each of the clerks' offices.

This is not to say, however, that all these office-holders looked upon him as their trusted friend. Indeed, a fair number did not and were apt, so to speak, to button up their pockets when they saw him coming. But George Uppard was impervious to rebuffs and by sheer forcefulness of character nearly always got his way, which was all he was concerned about. Contacts, knowing the right people, was all important to him and it mattered not that the assistance he obtained was often given with a minimum of grace or goodwill. As long as you never actually rubbed someone up the wrong way, it was his experience that they would generally help you, however grudgingly, simply because most people do not like saying 'no' to a request for a favour, whatever their private opinion of the supplicant. Though supplicant was hardly the word to describe Uppard's thrusting behaviour.

It was to South London Magistrate's Court that he made his way on the morning on which the discovery of Robin Appleman's murder was made.

One of Slatter's regular clients had been picked up the night before and charged with burglary. The police would be asking for a remand in custody and Uppard knew that they were hoping to be able to pin a number of further charges on him before the case was listed for hearing. The client was particularly anxious to obtain bail and Uppard, after a quick word on the telephone with Adrian Slatter, had managed at almost no notice at all to arrange for counsel to come along and make the application for bail.

The greater part of his time as Slatter's chief clerk was spent in this way. Instructing Counsel, often at the entrance to the Court, and telling the client what, and what not, to do and say. Hence the essential need for useful contacts at every Court.

'Use your phone a moment, Harry,' he said to the jailer at South London as he swept through the door and made his way to the instrument on the table over in a corner.

'S'pose so,' P.C. Grindley said without enthusiasm.

Uppard made his call, which was to another Magistrates' Court to say that he would be there by eleven thirty and would they please keep his case back till he arrived, and came over to where P.C. Grindley was busy examining his own list of charges and remands for that morning.

'What are you in?' the jailer enquired morosely. He was one of those who had no affection for Uppard and resented his sweeping assumption of favours, but had never felt embattled enough to deny them.

'Let's have a squint at your list, Harry. Yes, that's mine, Hall, number eight. I've got Counsel coming, Stanley Wood.'

'What for?'

'To apply for bail.'

'You haven't a hope.'

'We'll see. Who's sitting, anyway?'

'Mr Preece.'

'Pity. I'd have preferred old Bishopleigh.'

'Of course you would.'

'Anyway, there's always the Judge in Chambers if Preece refuses bail.'

P.C. Grindley grunted. 'If Hall can afford to instruct your firm *and* have counsel along here just on a bail application, that convinces me he ought to be kept in custody.'

'Why?'

'Because if he's let out, the next thing we'll hear will be he's living it up in Acapulco or one of those places.'

Uppard laughed indulgently. 'You're a hard man, Harry. Patsy Hall's not a bad chap. He just happens to be one of those unfortunates on whom the police have a particular down. They don't give him a chance.' He glanced across at the door through which there was constant traffic. 'Ah, here's Sergeant Pickin. I gather he's in charge of the case. Let me know when they bring Hall over from the station. I want to have a word with him before you stick him into Court.'

P.C. Grindley grunted and George Uppard went across to buttonhole Detective Sergeant Pickin.

'Hello,' Pickin said coolly, 'I didn't expect to see you here this morning.'

'Why not?'

'I thought you'd have more important things to attend to.'

'Do me a favour and stop talking in riddles.'

Sergeant Pickin eyed him suspiciously as Uppard's own expression became suddenly guarded.

'The murder.'

'What murder?'

'You mean to say you haven't heard?'

'I've heard nothing.'

'A barrister was murdered in his Chambers last night.'

'There are still enough left.'

'I'm serious.'

'So am I! What barrister in which Chambers and why has it got anything to do with me?'

Detective Sergeant Pickin shook his head in apparent embarrassment.

'I only heard about it just as I was leaving the station five minutes ago ... Someone had caught it on the grapevine. I don't really know that I ought to say any more ... I assumed you'd know.'

George Uppard's manner became bleakly hostile.

'Well, you've just bloody well got to after making all those insinuating remarks! What's the barrister's name?'

'I wasn't told his name. He's in some case your firm's

concerned with.' Sergeant Pickin gulped uncomfortably. 'It could be the Manion case, I think.'

'Do you mean James Geddy?'

'His pupil.'

'Appleman?'

'I didn't hear the name.'

'Appleman's been murdered in Chambers, is that it?'

Pickin nodded, watching Uppard with a mixture of awe and professional observation, while he rehearsed and recorded in his mind the conversation which had just taken place.

It was several seconds before Uppard made any reply. Then he said, '*Now* I understand why you're surprised to see me here this morning.' His face broke into a crooked smile. 'I may want you as my witness, mayn't I?'

*   *   *

Alan Dixon sat glowering at the square of partition wall behind his small, untidy desk. He was glad that he had his back to the rest of the room, even though the other three occupants were out and he had the place to himself. Sitting with his back to everyone, at least, provided him with as much privacy as was possible in a shared room.

He was worried about Sheila; a condition made worse by his powerlessness to do anything about it. All he could do was hope that she was coping all right with the police. She should be able to, but one simply could not predict how anyone would react under pressure. Of course, she might not find herself under any pressure, but he had his doubts about that. Doubts which sprang from a general mistrust of the police and of the wiles he suspected they employed in the course of an investigation.

Sheila knew a fair number of police officers through their coming to Chambers for conferences with barristers briefed to prosecute in various cases. She was given to tease him for his mistrust and tell him what cheerful and amusing men most of them were. Much nicer and more fun than a number of his colleagues, she would say when she specially wanted to provoke him.

He glowered harder at the unoffending wall as he re-called some of the occasions on which they had picked at this particular bone.

And there was another thing, he thought savagely: why did she insist on continuing to work at 4 Mulberry Court when she was aware that he would sooner she left and got a job elsewhere? Well, he knew the answer to that, too. Feminine obstinacy. And here again she was apt to taunt him about his feelings towards barristers, saying that he really ought not to reveal such an inferiority complex where they were concerned.

It just showed how little she really knew him, he re-flected in a moment of scourging self-pity, for he certainly had no feelings of inferiority about them. He merely dis-liked them. It was they who were insufferably superior, not he pathetically inferior. It annoyed him that Sheila could not, or would not, see this.

It was, however, to him, and not to any toffee-nosed bar-rister, that she had turned this time. And thank God for that, too!

'Hello, Alan, I didn't know you was in this morning or I'd 'ave come along earlier.' It was the girl who wheeled round a trolley, morning and afternoon, from which she served coffee in willow-pattern paper cups to anyone want-ing an additional excuse to stop work for a short time.

'I had to stay in for a phone call,' he said, glancing at her over his shoulder.

'Want a cup, Alan love?' she asked, at the same time reaching for a cup. She called everyone, apart from the directors by their first names. The directors were usually 'dear', but the chairman always got a 'sir'.

'Please.'

She brought the coffee over to where he was sitting and put it down on his desk.

'You feeling all right?' she said gazing at him intently.

'Yes, I'm all right.'

'You got beads of sweat on your upper lip and you're a

funny sort of colour.'

'It's a bit stuffy in here, that's all.'

She sniffed the air loudly. 'T'aint warm in 'ere to my thinking. I expect you're sickening for something. Anyway, drink up your coffee, it'll make you feel better.'

'I tell you I feel fine. There's nothing wrong with me at all.'

'Well, you should know...'

'I do.'

His tone had become testier and she gave him a puzzled look. 'You got beads of sweat on your forehead now,' she remarked decisively, 'and don't tell me it's anything to do with my coffee because it's neither strong nor hot enough to harm a new-born baby's skin.' She put her face closer to his. 'And you really are a funny colour, you know, love!'

Alan got up quickly. 'I'll go and take a breath of fresh air outside,' he said, pushing past her almost roughly.

She watched him stride from the room, then picked the cup off his desk and threw it in the waste container on the lower shelf of her trolley.

' 'E may be a nice-looking boy, 'e's always been a funny one, too,' she murmured to herself, as she prepared to follow him out. 'It's 'is sort can give you the creeps. It's them eyes, always so bloody angry-looking.'

*   *   *

The judge and counsel had embarked on a small discussion of their own as to the applicability, or otherwise, of the judgment in some other case to the facts pertaining to Manion's.

While they did so, Manion remained standing in the witness-box. For a time he listened to the exchange of views, knowing that his future might be considerably affected by the outcome, but then his attention drifted away as the argument became more and more unreal and concerned itself less with Manion than with that much revered legal figure 'the reasonable man'.

He leaned back against the wooden pillar which helped

to support the roof over the witness box. More like a lid it was really.

He had originally had doubts about James Geddy. He had never heard of him and had wanted Slatter to brief a barrister whose name was generally connected with defending big-time criminals. But, eventually, Adrian Slatter had persuaded him that Geddy was the right man for the case and this had certainly been borne out by his handling of the defence. Mind you, he had not liked him as a person on the showing of their two or three brief meetings, but he recognised that this was largely a question of mutual hostility.

Indeed, after the first and longest conference, he had told his solicitor flatly that he would not have him as his counsel. He had found him cold and unsympathetic to the point of rudeness. Adrian Slatter had laughed and reminded him that he, Manion, was similarly regarded by a good many people. And so, not without a characteristic display of his own brand of gracelessness, he had accepted Geddy. Now he was glad that he had. The case had gone well, the prosecution had been trounced and there seemed a very good chance that the trial should end with his complete acquittal. It better had if Adrian Slatter knew which side his bread was buttered!

As these thoughts passed through his mind, he had been looking at Geddy whose profile was towards him as Counsel stood facing the judge. The tall, lean figure and the long, narrow face, whose grave expression was accentuated by the wig which he wore tilted slightly forward like a Guards officer's cap. He had an air of heavy mourning about him and Manion guessed that his pupil's death must be the cause. It certainly was something out of the ordinary, even in Frank Manion's book, when barristers were murdered in their Chambers. Some of the boys would find a few laughs there all right!

Geddy shifted slightly and Manion's gaze moved on to the new young barrister sitting in the row behind. He smothered a desire to smile as he amused himself with the reflection that one got himself murdered, but a replacement popped up the very next day. This one appeared a much smoother type whose pleasant looks were not distorted by the absurd get-up. Some barristers managed to look rather distinguished when robed, but they were usually the older ones whose features could do with a bit of assistance. Most of the younger ones looked plain daft, Manion thought. Certainly, the murdered chap had! His wig was too large so that it appeared to cascade down either side of his head and his gown looked like something picked off a rubbish dump.

He became aware that David was staring back at him and he allowed his gaze to travel on. To Adrian Slatter sitting at the solicitors' table in the well of the Court, his face masked by a hand held to his forehead as he wrote in the margin of a document which lay open in front of him. His papers were scattered over far more than his share of the table and it was lucky that there was not more than one defending solicitor involved in the case.

Manion's expression was one of thoughtful appraisal as he watched his solicitor writing. There had been times recently when Slatter had seemed to overlook the requirements of his position. So far as Manion was concerned, he was no different from any other employee, save that he was rather better paid. Manion certainly had no time for the niceties of a professional relationship. Adrian Slatter was there to provide him with a service and to manipulate the law, as necessary, in meeting his demands.

In fact, he felt quite a friendly bond with his solicitor, and liked him in his own way. And if he was given to occasional outbursts of petulance when Manion's behaviour was more outrageous or condescending than usual, this was only to be expected and never seriously threatened their relationship. On the whole, Manion felt he knew just how far he could push Adrian Slatter. In one word, he knew how to *handle* him.

Nevertheless, his arrest and trial had introduced a new element into the relationship and had imposed strains not previously experienced. The balance had been disturbed to

Manion's disadvantage and he didn't like the new situation.

A man on trial and facing imprisonment is not in the same bargaining position as one ruling his own potent and undisputed empire.

In Manion's case, bargain was a misnomer. He generally forced others to do what he wanted. Sometimes he was unsuccessful. But bargains as such held little appeal for him. They were a sign of weakness. Unfortunately, like Samson, though not to the same disastrous extent, his strength had become sapped. For several weeks now, ever since his arrest, he had been like a man manacled.

He gripped the edge of the witness-box and let his gaze roam over the whole Courtroom. Pygmies! that's what they all were, including the judge dolled up in his scarlet and ermine.

His grip on the ledge tightened. By God, he would out-Samson Samson in pulling a temple down all round their puny ears should the jury convict him! And time was inexorably running out, with little he could now effectively do but await events. He seethed inwardly with a sudden overwhelming sense of impotence . . .

He heard James Geddy's voice coming as from a great distance and realised that his examination-in-chief was under way again.

He gave his head a small, quick shake as though to clear it of the black thoughts which had been stealthily laying siege to his mind. Then focusing his gaze on his counsel, he said in his quiet, unimpassioned voice, 'I'm sorry, but would you mind repeating the question?'

VII

At five o'clock that evening, everyone gathered in Philip Quant's room, which happened to be the largest in Chambers. He shared it with two others, one of whom had built up a substantial circuit practice in the West Country and whose appearances at 4 Mulberry Court became fewer and farther between, and the other who had recently broken a leg and who was reading briefs at home against the day when he could manage to hobble around the Courts.

Martin Ainsworth had earlier consulted the more senior members of Chambers, as a result of which Donald had been invited to attend, but not Stephen or Sheila.

There were about ten people present in all, about half of whom found chairs while the remainder draped themselves against pieces of furniture as comfortably as they could.

Anthea Rayner sat ensconced in the best chair and David and Holly perched on the narrow window seat behind Philip Quant's desk.

Martin Ainsworth stood over against the fireplace, one arm outflung along the mantelpiece.

He eyed the assembled company, and said, 'I don't think there's anyone else to come, is there?'

Everyone glanced about him with a grave air.

'What about Tony, isn't he coming?' Anthea enquired.

It was Donald who immediately spoke up. 'Mr Roberts is up at Norwich Assizes. He won't be back until the day after to-morrow.'

'Norwich Assizes finished two or three weeks ago,' Quant said in a contentious voice.

'It's a Special Assize,' Donald replied, a trifle sharply.

'Well, if we've sorted out Norwich Assizes, shall we begin?' Ainsworth said.

'I didn't know they were holding a Special Assize at Norwich,' Quant remarked to Anthea, who was sitting beside him.

'You do now,' she said severely without looking at him.

'May I start, Philip?'

'Oh, er . . . yes, please go ahead. I didn't realise you were waiting for me . . .'

'I thought it'd be as well,' Martin Ainsworth began, 'if we held a Chambers meeting. We don't have very many and happily we have never before had to meet in the tragic circumstances which have dictated this meeting. Perhaps I ought to begin by telling you of the various things I've done in my role as head of Chambers.

'I have written a letter to Robin's parents expressing our grief. This does not, of course, preclude anyone writing their own personal letter of condolence. Indeed, I imagine a number of you will wish to do that, anyway.' There were some nods and he went on, 'I have formally informed the Inn of Robin's murder since it took place on their premises. Though it would be more truthful to say that the Inn, in the person of the Under-Treasurer, has informed itself of the situation. Colonel Forster arrived in Chambers very soon after the police got here. But in addition to that, I went round to see him about an hour ago to give him a progress report.'

'I think that's what we'd all like to have, Martin,' Quant said, glancing round the room as though to rally opinion. 'A progress report.'

Ainsworth frowned. Though barristers spend a good deal of time in forensic interruptions of one another, they seldom take kindly to being on the receiving end.

'In fact,' he went on in an even tone, 'I have no progress to report. If the police are close to making an arrest, they have not taken me into their confidence, but I doubt very much whether they are. They have spent most of the day here, they've asked a lot of questions and they've interviewed most of those whom they seem to think can help them in their enquiries. And they're coming back in half an hour to interview those of you whom they've not yet had an opportunity of seeing.'

'I don't know that they're going to be able to see me,' Quant interjected. 'I've got a lot of work.'

'I told Roffey,' Ainsworth said in a slightly raised tone, 'that I was sure every member of the Chambers would co-operate in any way he could.' He looked at the faces all turned in his direction. 'I did not tell Roffey so, but, in fact, I regard it as everyone's duty to do what they can to assist the police. The sooner this case is solved the happier for all

of us. Until it has been, we must inevitably live under a
cloud of rumour and suspicion...'

'Really, Martin!' Quant exclaimed. 'Isn't that being
rather melodramatic? Surely no one's suggesting that
Robin Appleman was murdered by anyone in Chambers?'

'I'm neither suggesting it, nor am I counter-suggesting
it,' Ainsworth replied coldly. 'I'm merely stating what
seems to me to be the inevitable implication. Does anyone
else think I'm being melodramatic, as Philip puts it?'

'I don't,' Anthea said trenchantly. 'I trust the murderer
won't be found in our midst. I sincerely believe that he
won't. But, as seen by the outside world, of course we're all
under a cloud.'

'Some of us probably more than others,' James Geddy
said grimly. 'When Roffey interviewed me at lunchtime, it
was quite apparent from his questions that he regarded me
as a possible suspect.'

'I've never heard anything so bloody silly, if you'll excuse
the colloquialism,' Quant said. 'O.K., we're all suspects
until our movements are checked, but it then becomes obvious to the police that none of us had the opportunity, let
alone any motive.'

'Why do you say, none of us had the opportunity,
Philip?' Anthea asked. 'We all have keys to Chambers. Any
one of us *could*, I imagine, have returned stealthily...'

'But why? For what reason?'

'I wasn't talking about motive, only opportunity. I imagine once the police can establish the motive, they'll know
who did it.'

'What is this, the Temple sect of masochists! I bet each
one of us has a copper-bottomed alibi for when the murder
was committed, so let's stop sounding like a lot of unholy
martyrs.'

'When was the murder committed?' James Geddy asked
quietly, as everyone suddenly turned in Philip Quant's
direction.

'Some time fairly soon after we all left Chambers last
night, wasn't it?'

For a few seconds, no one spoke. Then Ainsworth said, 'I'm not sure that the police have yet established the time of death.'

'Well, if it wasn't *then*, what the hell was Appleman doing in Chambers in the middle of the night?' Quant demanded. 'Or at whatever hour it was, if it wasn't then?'

'I suggest that we don't embark on sterile speculation,' Ainsworth said firmly. 'I simply repeat that, in my view – and I trust it is one which most of you share – these next few days may prove difficult and embarrassing. It is important, I think, that we should behave with dignity and circumspection so far as the world outside is concerned and I would particularly ask that you should steer clear of the press.' He gave a small, wry smile. 'That, I realise, is easier said than done, but even though you are waylaid or rung up you can still refuse to talk about the case. Not only can, but *should*. The last thing we want, on top of all else, is the suggestion that we've hampered the police by giving unofficial press conferences.'

'The press often help to solve crimes,' Quant observed loftily.

'So it often tells us,' Ainsworth replied. 'However, if it's to be so in this case, let the police be the informants, not any member of these Chambers.'

'They certainly won't get anything out of me,' Anthea remarked to the room at large. Holly gave David a surreptitious wink.

Martin Ainsworth's gaze once more took in the assembled company. 'Has anyone got anything further to say before we disperse? Chief Superintendent Roffey will be back in a few minutes and I'd ask you all to hang on in Chambers until you've found whether or not he wants to see you.'

The meeting broke up. One or two people drifted out of the room, but others coalesced into small groups.

'I imagine Martin or someone has told the police about Appleman and Sheila?' Quant said to Anthea.

'I've no idea, Philip,' she replied in an anything but

encouraging tone.

'Because if not, somebody ought to,' he went on. 'It's a pretty obvious line of enquiry for the police.'

Anthea Rayner looked at him sharply. Despite her disdain for what she regarded as Philip Quant's vulgar zest for gossip, her curiosity was aroused, 'You're not suggesting Sheila had anything to do with Robin's death?'

'I'm not suggesting she killed him,' he said keenly, 'but what about that jealous boy-friend of hers?'

'I've never set eyes on him. Or rather, that's all I have done on a couple of occasions. I certainly didn't know he was jealous. Where do you get that from?'

Quant grinned at her. 'Oh, I happened to hear Sheila talking on the phone to a girl-friend a few weeks ago. It was the middle of the morning and I went along to the clerks' room to get something and Sheila was having a fine old natter. I couldn't help overhearing what she was saying. It was all about her boy-friend Alan and how he had recently kicked up the hell of a rumpus at a restaurant because he thought some chap was giving her the glad eye. It wasn't the first time either, she remarked to whoever it was she was talking to.'

'And who *was* she talking to, Philip?' Anthea asked nastily, 'I'm sure you overheard that, too.'

'Someone called Brenda,' he replied unabashed. 'He looks that type, too,' he went on. 'Quite a good-looking chap, but with an intense expression as though he's always expecting trouble and is more than ready to deal with it.'

Anthea shook her her head slowly. 'You know, Philip, this is entirely speculation on your part and dangerous speculation at that.'

'In what way dangerous?'

'You have absolutely no evidence that this young man had anything whatsoever to do with Robin's death, and to talk as though he may be a murderer is not only irresponsible but dangerous, in my view.'

'Of course I haven't any evidence, my dear Anthea. That's a matter for the police. All I'm saying is that

Sheila's boy-friend had a motive and, more than likely, an opportunity as well.'

'You don't even know that he had a motive,' she said scornfully. 'Good heavens, jealousy has to be almost a form of insanity before boy-friends commit murder on that score!'

He looked at her in amused pity. 'And that from you, who has been practising in the criminal courts for a quarter of a century! You know quite well it isn't true! You know as well as I do that simple sexual jealousy is one of the commonest motives for murder among the under twenty-fives.'

'I still think you should be careful what you say about Sheila's boy-friend.'

'I don't want to say anything, provided I'm assured that the police have been tipped off. After that, it's up to them. Anyway, I'll go and ask Martin now.'

As Philip Quant left her side, James Geddy came up. Anthea gave him a small smile.

'I expect you're feeling wretched,' she said in a sympathetic tone.

He nodded. 'It's not much fun for any of us.'

'Philip doesn't seem too affected,' she said.

'Oh, Philip always enjoys a human drama. It's his strength and his weakness as a criminal advocate. But he doesn't mean any harm.'

'You'll be saying next that his heart's in the right place,' Anthea remarked dryly. 'Anyway, to change the subject, how's the Manion trial going?'

Geddy grimaced. 'I shall be glad when it's over, whatever the result. It never was my favourite case and now...' His tone indicated a suppressed vehemence as he went on, '... And now it fills me with complete and utter revulsion.'

'That's understandable,' Anthea said calmly.

James Geddy passed a hand across his forehead. 'Do you mind if I use your room this evening? Couldn't face sitting in mine...'

90

VIII

David and Holly had stood listening to their pupil-masters without joining in the conversation. Afterwards Holly had submitted herself to interview by one of Roffey's minions who had arrived by that time. It had not taken long as she had been able to satisfy him that she knew nothing which could further the enquiry or which they had not already been told. David had made a short statement to the police at lunchtime when Roffey and Chisett had interviewed James Geddy at the Old Bailey.

So far as the two pupils had been concerned, it had been a question of stating the hour at which they had left Chambers the previous evening; who was still there; no, they had not returned; and no, they were unable to cast any light on the mystery of Robin Appleman's death.

As soon as Holly had completed her statement, she and David left to go home.

'I'll pick you up in about an hour's time,' he said, as they parted company at Charing Cross Underground Station, she to journey on to Earl's Court and he to change trains and head for Regent's Park which was the nearest station to the flat he shared with his brother.

Holly had a tiny flat at the top of a solid Victorian house just off the Earl's Court Road.

She was ready and waiting when the bell which was operated from the street door rang. She looked out of the window and saw David's Triumph T.R.6 parked outside.

'Coming,' she called into the intercom as she picked up an ancient raincoat. She was wearing a pair of cherry-red slacks and a black roll-top sweater, which made her look very different from Holly Childersley, barrister-at-law.

David, too, had changed and was dressed in almost identical fashion, save that his slacks were the colour of french

91

mustard and he had a short fawn motoring coat with huge patch pockets over his sweater.

He greeted her with a conspiratorial grin and opened the car door for her to get in.

A ten-minute drive brought them to the street in which Robin had lived.

'Best to park round the corner, I think,' he said, his tone betraying a feeling of slight nervousness.

Holly nodded. 'Yes, let's,' she replied, her own tone sounding spuriously eager.

A few seconds later she shrank into the shadows while he locked the car doors. The sky was overcast and there was that smell of dampness in the air which is common for a November evening in London. The end of the road in which they had parked was dominated by the huge, dark outline of Lots Road Power Station. It looked sinister and forbidding, and Holly shivered.

'All right?' David enquired, linking his arm through hers.

'Fine,' she lied, pressing herself closer to his side.

'Relax,' he said, gently. 'We don't want to draw attention to ourselves, so we just walk along quite naturally, O.K.?'

She gave a quick nod.

There was a pub on the corner, from which friendly noises were coming forth, but the street into which they turned was empty. A hundred yards farther up, buses and cars passed across at an intersection. It was only eight o'clock, but to both of them it seemed much later. They felt they had suddenly entered a different world, not merely a fresh postal district. An unfamiliar world in which unknown dangers might lurk.

'This is the baker's,' Holly suddenly whispered, as they reached an unlit shop window. 'Down here.'

As she spoke, she shot down a narrow passage which ran beside the shop. A few yards down, they came to a door, let into the side of the shop at the rear.

'This is Robin's door,' she said in another whisper. She bent down and fished around with her fingers in a crevice at one side of the doorstep. When she stood up, she was holding a key.

David took it from her and opened the door. They stepped inside and found themselves at the foot of a narrow flight of stairs.

'The door to his flat is at the top,' Holly said in a still hushed voice, as David started to go up.

There was a small landing and she once more knelt down and retrieved a key, with which David opened the second door.

They were about to pass inside when he happened to shine his torch down the stairs. 'What's that on the floor down there?' he asked.

His tone made Holly jump. 'Looks like a letter,' she said, trying to keep a slight note of hysteria out of her voice.

'I didn't notice it when we came in,' he said. A couple of seconds later, he had fetched it and returned upstairs again. 'Yes, it is a letter addressed to Robin and posted yesterday. It's postmarked Taunton. Probably from his parents.'

David eyed the envelope speculatively.

'You're not going to open it?' Holly said anxiously.

'Let's look around the flat,' he said, putting the letter into one of the large pockets of his coat.

They were standing in a narrow hallway off which there were three doors, all closed. While Holly remained standing nervously just inside the front door, David opened each door in turn and shone his torch carefully into the rooms. One was a kitchen, not much larger than a telephone kiosk and next to it was a small bathroom with an old-fashioned hot-water heater suspended over one end of the bath. Both rooms evidenced Robin's haphazard and disorderly domestic routine. The kitchen contained a large number of unwashed utensils. There was a jar of instant coffee minus its lid and a bag of white sugar with a hole in its side from which the contents had spilt on the table. The bathroom was equally squalid with tubes of this and that without their caps in place, a rusty-looking razor and a shaving brush whose hairs were worn almost to the bone handle.

The third door led into the bed-cum-sitting-room. It was over the front of the shop and looked out on the street. David walked across and drew the curtains. Holly watched anxiously as he tried, without success, to make them meet in the middle.

'We'll still have to make do with the torch,' he said. 'Bit risky to switch on the light!'

Holly nodded a vigorous assent. Standing with his back to the window, David shone his torch round the room.

'Poor old Robin,' he said, 'he didn't live very comfortably, did he?'

'It didn't look as cheerless as this the time he asked me to supper,' Holly replied with a small shiver. She glanced at the rumpled, unmade bed and blinked as tears began to prick her eyes. 'He must have got up in a hurry yesterday morning. He didn't have time to make his bed. It somehow brings home the suddenness of his death, seeing the bed like that.'

As he stood flashing his torch about the room, David, too, felt his emotions starting to engulf his self-control. A lump formed in his throat as he again remembered the angry and taunting words he had thrown at Robin the previous evening in Chambers. Previous evening! In one way, it felt more like a hundred years ago. He swallowed hard and compressed his lips and was glad that Holly couldn't see his face.

'It must have been pretty lonely coming back to this every evening,' he said dully. 'If one had realised . . .'

'We'd better not get too sentimental, David.'

'You're right!'

'Though I started it, I'm afraid. It was seeing the bed . . .'

'Did he have any friends, apart from people in Chambers?'

'I never heard him mention any, but he didn't talk much about his life outside. I wouldn't have thought that he regarded anyone in Chambers as a real friend.'

'I think he liked you and me.'

'But we weren't his friends, David, not as you and I mean it.'

'I suppose not.'

While they had been talking David had been moving cautiously about the room, opening drawers and peering into a cupboard. He was unsure what he was looking for, but there was certainly nothing which arrested his attention. The whole idea of their coming was beginning to seem pointless and futile. It had been conceived as a gesture of loyalty and solidarity and, at the time, had stimulated their minds with its promise of mild adventure. It was as though they were the faithful followers of a martyred leader.

But now standing in the eerie atmosphere of Robin's fraily lit room, surrounded by sordid reminders of his mortality, the enterprise had lost any romance it ever had.

'Shine the torch over there by the bed,' Holly said suddenly.

David did as he was bidden.

'On the floor by the head of the bed,' Holly directed. 'His case has gone,' she said. 'He had an attaché case in which he kept all his papers,' she went on. 'When I came to supper with him, there was a photograph he wanted to show me and he put the attaché case on the bed and opened it. I remember noticing how full it was. There was also a diary in it, because Robin held it up, and asked me if I kept one.'

'Well, there's no attaché case in this room now,' David said after a short search.

'I wonder what can have happened to it.'

'I imagine the police must have taken it.'

'The police!'

'They must have been here in the course of the day. It'd be part of the routine. They'd have used the keys they found in Robin's pocket.' He gave Holly a small grin in the semi-darkness. 'I don't suppose they knew of the secret nooks where he kept the spares.' He paused. 'Incidentally, why do you think he told you?'

It was several seconds before Holly replied and she turned away from him when she spoke. 'I think he hoped I'd . . . I'd make greater use of the flat than, in fact, I wanted to.'

'You mean he wanted you to shack up here with him.'

'He never said so in that many words, but there were hints . . .'

'Of which mention of the hiding-place of the keys was one?'

'I took it as such.'

'Well, well!' David remarked. Holly turned and looked at him. 'I felt sorry for Robin, just as you did. But pity isn't a very sound basis for any sort of relationship and it was the last thing that Robin wanted.'

'But what about Sheila and him?'

'What about them?'

'Did he go straight from you to her?'

'It wasn't a question of that. I made it quite clear I wasn't interested in him that way as soon as I got the message.'

'But Sheila mayn't have! Was he upset when you gave him the bum's rush?'

'Not unduly. I think he may already have set his sights on Sheila. I suspect that he only made a tentative pass at me because we were fellow-pupils.'

'He was the sort of person, too, who'd have felt it in the proper order of things to have a barrister girl-friend.'

'Perhaps, though I don't find that very flattering.'

'If it helps, let me say that I think you're very attractive, despite the fact you're a barrister.'

Holly smiled at him. 'I'll work that out some time.'

'I'll help you,' he said, pulling her suddenly to him and kissing her. Releasing her several seconds later, he asked, 'Know what we're going to do now?' Holly's startled gaze flew to the bed. 'Steam open that letter,' he said.

This turned out to be a simple task as the flap of the envelope was barely secured, someone having evidently economised in saliva when sealing it.

David extracted the contents, a single sheet of blue

notepaper with the address hand-written at the top. It began: 'My dear Robin,' and he quickly turned to the end to see who had sent it. The final words were: 'From your ever-loving Mother'.

Holly stood beside him and read it at the same time as he held it in the light of his torch, rather as though they were sharing a carol sheet.

It read:

'My dear Robin,

We were glad to receive your letter, though disappointed that you won't be coming down for a weekend before Christmas. But if you're making friends up in London, that's nice. You must tell us about her when you come.

Dad hurt his back at work last week and the doctor has told him to take things easy. Rosemary has a new young man. He works in the Council offices and is called Geoffrey. He seems a nice young fellow and is in the architect's department. If he can't be a barrister, I quite fancy an architect for a son-in-law!

Uncle George looked in the other evening and says why don't you come to the local Assizes as there are too many foreigners and a local boy would take all the work. He'd been talking to someone who works at the Court.

I can't always read your writing nowadays. It seems to have got scrawly. Perhaps because you have to do so much. Anyway, I can't read the name of the person you're in trouble with. Sometimes one can't avoid rows, but it's always best to do so if you can. I'm not a barrister, son, but I've lived longer than you have and would always advise anyone to avoid trouble if they can. You don't say what the row was about. Perhaps you were tactless the way you sometimes are. Anyway, the best thing is to make it up as soon as you can.

Time to close – Dad and Rosemary send love. From your ever-loving Mother.'

Holly was the first to speak. 'She sounds nice. She was obviously very fond of Robin.'

David seemed preoccupied. 'Who'd he had a row with, I wonder?' he murmured. 'Could it have been Philip?'

'Philip Quant?' Holly asked in surprise.

'Yes,' David said and went on to explain the curious hostility that his pupil-master had shown towards Robin.

'But what on earth could Philip and Robin have had a row about? They scarcely came into contact with each other.'

'I know, but something must have happened between them. Personally, I get along fine with Philip, but he's a bit of an odd man out. I never feel that Martin Ainsworth and James Geddy and the others of that seniority really like him.'

'Anthea certainly turned on him at that meeting this evening.'

'He has a slightly malicious streak. I've several times had the impression that he's not averse to stirring up a bit of trouble and then standing back and watching the results.'

'But how did Robin get across him?'

'I've no idea, but I feel he must have been referring to Philip in his letter home.'

'Even if he was, it can't have had anything to do with Robin's death.'

'That's something we can't know, is it?'

'You're not suggesting that Philip murdered Robin?' Holly asked in astonishment. 'He's your pupil-master.'

'I don't follow the logic of that! Robin was my fellow-pupil, but that doesn't mean I couldn't have murdered him. Save that I didn't. Anyway, we can at least follow the matter up.'

'How?'

'By paying a visit to Robin's parents. We could go down on Saturday for the day. It would be a natural thing to do, to go and express our condolences in person.'

'What are you going to do with the letter?'

'Re-seal it and leave it where I found it.'

'You'd better wipe off your fingerprints first.'

David grinned. 'Not many girls would have thought of that.'

'Not many girls,' Holly remarked dryly, 'have seen someone convicted largely on the evidence of a fingerprint on a letter. One of Anthea's clients was the other day.'

'I'm hungry,' David said as they made their way back down the narrow staircase. 'Let's go and put our fingerprints on some knives and forks.'

The keys were carefully replaced in their hiding-places and they crept furtively down the passage-way towards what suddenly seemed like freedom. The street was as empty of people as when they arrived and they were soon back at the car.

A few minutes later they were in the King's Road and, not long after, sitting in a small Italian restaurant which was known to David.

Later – very much later – as he drove himself home, he looked back on the evening as from a great distance.

It had taken a small adventure for him to see Holly as a rather delicious member of her own sex. He had always thought her attractive, but had tended to regard her solely as a professional colleague despite a fair amount of evidence that she lacked the necessary toughness to survive the competition of the Bar.

He smiled ruefully as he reflected on his often professed determination to eschew the Bar as a hunting-ground for girl-friends.

But the alchemy of poor old Robin's melancholy surroundings seemed to have worked a change.

As he lay in bed, however, his last thoughts before dropping off to sleep were not romantic, but of an unknown murderer who now seemed closer to them all than he had originally wanted to believe.

IX

Detective Chief Superintendent Roffey arrived at head-quarters at half past eight the next morning.

He looked in the pink of condition and the fresh tang of his after-shave lotion contrasted agreeably with the rather staler odours of the building.

He acknowledged the 'good mornings' which punctuated his progress to his room by the use of his umbrella. A half-turn of his wrist moved the ferrule through an upward angle of thirty degrees and indicated that the matutinal greeting had been received and was reciprocated.

On arrival in his room, he removed his bowler and, after examining it judiciously, hung it on a peg behind the door. The umbrella was stood in a small blue pot in a corner of the room and the carefully folded *Times* was laid on the desk.

He glanced at his watch. There was still ten minutes to go before he was due to see the Assistant Commissioner. He wondered if Detective Sergeant Chisett had arrived and was about to enquire when that officer came in.

'Good morning, sir.'

'Good morning,' Roffey's tone was as cool as a royal handshake.

'I've been through all the stuff we took from Appleman's flat yesterday, sir. His diary is the only item of interest.'

'You have it there?'

Sergeant Chisett handed him the red notebook which had been tucked beneath his arm. 'I've flagged the interesting bits. See what you think of them, sir!'

Roffey took the notebook and sat down at his desk. Before opening it, however, he pulled a pair of black horn-rimmed spectacles out of his breast pocket, which he proceeded to polish with a clean, folded handkerchief, while

Chisett watched him with a mixture of impatience and expectation.

At last he was ready to start reading and opened the diary at the first marker. Almost immediately he closed it again and reopened it at the beginning.

'All that early part deals with events before he began at Mulberry Court, sir. There's nothing of interest until about a month ago.'

But Roffey took no notice and began slowly turning the earlier pages. Sergeant Chisett let out a long, slow sigh. It was never any good trying to nudge his Chief Superintendent along a particular path. You had only to suggest something, for him, figuratively, to gaze in the other direction. He was quietly, but chronically, contrary.

Chisett pulled out a packet of cigarettes. 'Mind if I smoke, sir?'

Roffey was a non-smoker and was liable to react to the scattering of ash and butts in his room like a wary virgin to a pair of unzipped trousers.

'Go ahead,' he said without glancing up.

Sergeant Chisett lit his cigarette and pretended to look around for an ashtray in which to put the spent match.

'Don't strain your neck muscles,' Roffey said, still without looking up, 'there isn't an ashtray and you'll have to take your debris with you.'

'Sorry, sir, I'd forgotten you don't have one.' In an obscure way, Chisett felt he had scored a point. Roffey, for his part, knew exactly what his sergeant was feeling, but was unperturbed provided he did not drop ash all over the place. Except he would sooner he did not smoke at all, but he realised that was something beyond his control.

He reached the page to which Chisett had first directed his attention.

'About half-way down, sir,' Chisett said keenly. 'Where it begins, "Sheila's eyes are like liquid satin shot with flecks of sunshine."' He made a scoffing sound. 'Not when I saw her, they weren't! More like tarnished buttons in a blood-shot sauce! Anyway, sir, you see how he goes on about some of her other features, even though all above the navel. But it shows he was besotted with her. And then about two pages farther on, he refers to her young man, says he has a feeling she isn't as fond of him as she pretends, that she's grown tired of him because he's so possessive. That's the significant bit, sir, the reference to his possessiveness. It's the motive we've been looking for. That young man's certainly got something to hide, it stuck out a mile when we saw him yesterday. He was as tense as hell. Probably thought we were going to take him in there and then. Sheila had a key to Chambers so he had access. Access and motive. I think what probably happened was that Appleman made another pass at Sheila when they were the only two left in Chambers that evening. Possibly went a bit farther than usual. Tried to dirty his fingers, something like that. She took exception and told Dixon when he came to pick her up and he went back to Chambers to have it out with Appleman. They had a flaming row and in a fit of jealous rage, Dixon picks up that paperknife from the desk and stabs Appleman in the throat.' He paused as Roffey closed the diary and looked up. 'It all fits, sir. Don't you agree that's probably what happened?'

'No.'

Sergeant Chisett's jaw dropped. He had become quite carried away by his reconstruction of the crime, despite the absence of any responsive interest on the part of his audience. For Roffey had continued reading the entries in Robin's diary while Chisett had been gathering momentum. And now he had been halted by a cool, dispassionately uttered monosyllable.

'But it fits, sir,' he protested after a pause for recovery.

'I dare say it does. So do a number of other theories.'

'Well, what's your theory, sir?'

Roffey glanced at the gold watch on his left wrist.

'I have to go and see the A.C.,' he said. 'I'll give you a call as soon as I'm back. Meanwhile, find out if the lab have reached any preliminary conclusions about any of the exhibits.'

'They hardly will have yet, sir.'

Roffey nodded in an abstracted way. 'But find out.' Frowning, he scratched at something on the sleeve of his jacket. Then daintily licking the tip of one finger, he rubbed at the spot. 'Seem to have blood on my sleeve,' he remarked crossly.

'Probably from the p.m., sir,' Chisett said cheerfully and once more felt that he had scored a mark. Blood on his Chief Superintendent's clothing was bad enough without the suggestion that it had been acquired in a mortuary. He had noticed how careful Roffey had been, both there and at the scene, to leave his bowler and umbrella at a safe distance from possible contamination. Serve him right now if he had got some of the victim's blood on his sleeve.

Roffey was still rubbing and scratching the mark when he arrived outside the Assistant Commissioner's door.

'Ah! Come in and sit down, Roy,' the A.C. said briskly.

'I'm sorry I'm a bit late, sir, I was having a quick look through the diary we found at Appleman's flat.'

'Anything of significance in it?'

'Not to my mind. It confirms that he was infatuated with the Chambers typist – that's the girl, Sheila – but I don't personally think that has anything to do with his death.'

'But it might have?'

'Yes, it might have,' Roffey conceded in a tone intended to convey nothing more than his open-mindedness.

'But you clearly don't believe it did,' the A.C. added.

Roffey nodded and crossed one leg over the other, a pose he rarely adopted because of its creasing effect on trousers. The A.C. noted the change of position with interest. It usually prefaced one of his more oracular observations.

'To me, sir, the most significant thing is the absence of any fingerprints where you might expect to have found them.' He paused, uncrossed his legs and held up his left hand as he prepared to tick off the points of significance on his mental list. 'There were none on the weapon, none on the desk, none on the chair, none on the papers on the desk and none on the door.'

'Someone made a good job of wiping the place clean.'

'Exactly, sir. Why?'

'That's pretty obvious, isn't it? Why does any criminal stop to remove his prints! So as to avoid detection, of course!'

Roffey gave him a small, tolerant smile 'Yes, yes, sir, but why did the murderer take such special care in this case, sir?'

'You tell me, Holmes,' the A.C. said with a slight edge to his tone.

'Surely it must have been for one or two reasons. Either he has a criminal record and his fingerprints are on file or he comes within the very small category of persons who might naturally expect to be invited to give their prints for purposes of elimination.'

'You never know these days,' the A.C. remarked drily, 'but has anyone in those Chambers got a criminal record?'

'One of them has,' Roffey said with the self-satisfied air of one playing a difficult hand of bridge with recognised competence. 'It was a long time ago when he was still a student. He avoided paying his fare on the Underground and was fined £3.'

'Oh, is that all!' The A.C.'s tone was contemptuous.

'You say that, sir, but it was an offence involving moral turpitude. Not something which a professional man, like a barrister, cares to have hidden in his past. You never know when it won't pop out with uncomfortable results, if not worse.'

'And who is this criminal type living down his past at 4 Mulberry Court?'

'His name's Quant. Philip Quant.'

'Never heard of him. Not that that means much. Never heard of three quarters of these chaps whose names I see these days. Never heard of some of the judges.'

Roffey waited for this somewhat plaintive denunciation of the legal hierarchy to finish, then said, 'As far as I've been able to ascertain, sir, no one in Chambers knows about Quant's previous conviction.'

'You mean that no one admits to knowing?'

'Obviously I've not asked the direct question of anyone, but I've steered my interviews with members of Chambers so that I reckon I'd know if they knew.'

The A.C. grunted, apparently as much unimpressed by the information as by the intuitive instincts of his officer. 'Did Quant have any motive to murder Appleman?' he asked grudgingly.

Roffey awarded the question one of his superior smiles.

'If you'd asked me that twenty minutes ago, sir, I'd have had to have said none that I knew of. But there's rather an interesting entry in Appleman's diary which may throw a little light on that question. It's dated about two weeks ago.' He opened the diary towards the end.

The A.C. put out a hand. 'Let's see.'

'His writing's not very easy, sir. It may be simpler if I read the extract to you.'

The A.C. leaned back with an air of resignation. He would like one day to be present at a confrontation between Roffey and someone of equal vanity and contrariness. The trouble was that people always gave way to him simply because most of the occasions did not merit joining issue. Life was short and was sufficiently replete with sources of exhaustion without adding to them unnecessarily.

'It's an entry dated the twenty-third of October, sir. "How thankful I am that I'm not Philip Quant's pupil after what I know of him. Apart from anything else, James Geddy is much the better man, though David seems to get on all right with P.Q." That's a reference to David March, sir, who is Quant's pupil. And then five days later, there's this: "Q. can't stand my guts. Never misses any opportunity of snubbing or taunting me. He doesn't get many, fortunately, and is fairly careful about not doing it in front of others. The best thing is to try and keep out of his way. But that he of all people should behave this way . . ." ' Roffey looked up. 'He obviously wrote up his diary when he had time. The last entry is almost a week before his death.'

'You've not questioned Quant yet?'

'Not about this, sir. As I say, I only came across it a few minutes ago.'

The A.C. pursed his lips. 'Well, obviously he'll have to be asked about it, though I confess it doesn't sound to me like the seed of murder. Appleman and Quant didn't get on. Full stop. Lots of people don't get on . . .'

'But that bit, sir, about being glad he's not Quant's pupil after what he knows about him. That calls for some explanation.'

'The trouble is that the best person to explain it is dead.'

'But the next best is still alive.'

'Whether or not he *is* the next best depends on what there is to explain. You may yet have to requestion everyone in Chambers about relations between these two.'

'I'm expecting to have to do that, sir.'

'I wish you luck. If I know anything, you'll find they've closed ranks against you.'

'I trust I shall be able to show them where their duty lies,' Roffey said pompously. 'After all, this is a murder enquiry.'

The A.C. grunted. He doubted whether members of the Bar were, as a profession, any more susceptible to appeals to their sense of duty than haberdashers or stationmasters. He was generally cynical about human nature and considered that most of its impulses sprang from self-interest. There were honourable exceptions, but they were not usually met in the course of a criminal investigation.

'Did the p.m. tell you anything you didn't know before?' he asked.

Roffey frowned once more at his minutely bloodstained sleeve. 'No, sir. Cause of death was a stab wound of the neck. The carotid artery had been severed and the injury was consistent with having been caused by the silver paper-knife which Mr Geddy kept on his desk.'

'What degree of force was used?'

'It was a sudden, quick stab according to Professor Drayton.'

'How does he know it was quick?'

'Appleman was sitting in a chair which revolves and if it hadn't been sudden and quick, the inference is that he'd have spun away from the approaching weapon.'

The A.C. appeared to consider this.

'Was the blow struck from in front or behind?'

'From in front. Probably across the desk, his assailant facing him.'

'That doesn't sound very practicable.'

'It's quite a narrow desk, sir. It wouldn't present any obstacle to someone leaning over it. I've experimented and you could easily stab a person sitting in the chair on the other side. Professor Drayton holds the same opinion. We carried out a number of tests when he was at the scene.'

'So while Appleman is sitting at the desk, his murderer picks up the paperknife, leans across and stabs him.'

'Yes.'

'Therefore it's an inference that the murderer was in the room probably talking to him before the attack took place.'

'Yes, sir.'

'Then something was said or done which precipitated the stabbing,' the A.C. mused aloud. 'The question is what?' Roffey remained silent and after a short while, the A.C. said in a brisker tone, 'What about this solicitor's clerk, Uppard, he was the last known person to see Appleman alive, wasn't he?'

'Yes, sir.'

'Anything on *him*?'

'I've known Uppard a number of years, sir, and I wouldn't trust him to tell me the day of the week, but there's no evidence against him in respect of this murder.'

'What's he say?'

'That he arrived at Chambers some time after seven o'clock, that he knocked loudly on the outer door and entered and that as he did so Appleman appeared at the end of the passage. That it was Appleman who came to him and not the other way about and that he handed him the papers for Mr Geddy, turned round and departed. He says that they didn't exchange more than a dozen words and that he never got farther than the door to Chambers.'

'Where'd he go then?'

'Says he went to a pub in Southwark to meet a client.'

'Confirmed?'

'Yes.'

'It's one of those firms, is it?'

'Sir?'

'One of those firms where business is transacted in South London pubs?'

'Finster, Slatter & Co. have that sort of clientele, sir, and George Uppard is the sort of managing clerk you'd expect to find with them. He's tough, cunning, and unscrupulous, but not without an engaging streak.'

'Murder sounds right up his street.'

'No motive, sir.'

'But he was the last person to see the dead man alive.'

'Somebody has to be, sir!'

'I know *that*! What I am trying to say is that, more often than not, the last known person proves to be the last person in fact, i.e. the murderer.'

'I don't think it was Uppard, sir,' Roffey said obstinately.

The A.C. stared at him in silence for a moment and then looked away. Roffey waited a second, then stood up.

'If you'll excuse me, sir . . .'

'Still confident?' the A.C. enquired, focusing his gaze back on his Chief Superintendent.

'Certainly, sir, yes.'

'Where's your first port of call to-day?'

'I promised the Under-Treasurer of the Inn that I'd look in and let him know how my enquiries are going. The Benchers are naturally anxious to be kept in touch.'

'Naturally,' the A.C. said drily.

If Roffey noticed the faint note of mockery, he showed no sign of it. Funny, the A.C. reflected, how sycophantic he was towards the upper reaches of the legal profession when his respect for his own superiors was, at its highest, formal.

Nevertheless, he was still a shrewd and capable officer who usually solved his cases with a minimum of wasted effort.

The A.C. suddenly smiled at the door which Roffey had just closed behind him. He was wondering how his Chief Superintendent would react if the murderer should turn out to be no one less than one of Her Majesty's judges. The emotional predicament might prove fatal.

X

At the same time as the A.C. and Detective Chief Superintendent Roffey were conferring, so were Adrian Slatter and George Uppard.

Slatter was slumped in the chair behind his desk. His face had an unhealthy, puffy look about it and his eyes gave the appearance of having spent the night suspended over a wood fire.

George Uppard knew the signs well enough. His principal had been out on the tiles, which, in his case, meant drinking too much brandy in the small hours and ending up in someone else's bed. Probably one of his terrible old bags who could knock back the brandy at an even quicker rate. It was either one of them or some much younger country-type girl at whom he would make a strenuous and unsubtle pass.

Uppard could never understand why he didn't go for something in between the two. It was not as though he lacked the eligibility. He had reasonable looks and, as important in the particular field, reasonable dough.

'Well, I don't see that there's anything I can do, George,' Slatter said a trifle testily.

'I'm not asking you to do anything, Mr Slatter, sir, I'm just telling you what happened.'

Slatter knew that he had to step warily whenever his

chief clerk addressed him as 'Mr Slatter, sir'.

'You've no reason to think that your interview with Roffey was any different from anyone else's, even though you may be the last known person to have seen Robin Appleman alive.'

'That's why I must be a suspect and I don't like it.'

'I don't suppose you're any more of a suspect than half a dozen other people.'

'I don't want to be one at all.'

'Well, I'm sure you've got nothing to worry about. After all you had no motive for murdering him, did you?'

'No, Mr Slatter, sir, I did not have any motive.'

'There you are then! I don't know why you're in a fuss.'

'I'm not in a fuss, I'm merely narked at finding myself in the position through no fault of mine.'

'Look, George,' Slatter said, with an impatient squirm, 'if a tile falls off a roof, it's liable to hit someone in the street below. An innocent someone. It's not his fault that he happened to be there at that moment. It just happens to be the way the cookie crumbles.'

'I take good care to see that tiles don't fall on my head and, if cookies start crumbling in my vicinity, it's because I'm doing the crumbling.' His tone was flat and hard.

'Well, what do you suggest I do?'

'All I ask, Mr Slatter, sir, is that you back me up with the police.'

'Of course, in so far as I can.'

'Not just in so far as you can, but in so far as is necessary. Necessary, that is, to convince them I had nothing to do with the unfortunate Mr Appleman's death.'

Adrian Slatter stared at his clerk with a worried and puzzled expression.

'I don't know why you think they'll need convincing,' he said uncertainly.

'Nor do I – yet. It's just that I believe in preparing in advance.'

'Merely because you were the last person to see Robin

Appleman alive doesn't mean you murdered him.'

'It's nice of you to say so.'

Slatter closed his eyes. 'It's too early in the day for your sarcasm!' he said wearily. Opening them again he added, 'Anyway, you usually manage to have both ears to the ground, what have you picked up about the way Roffey's enquiries are going?'

'They seem to think it was an inside job, somebody connected with Chambers.'

'Any ideas who?'

Uppard shook his head. 'Who'd be your guess?'

'I don't make guesses of that sort. I just hope they catch the chap. I liked Appleman. It's still difficult to believe he's been murdered.'

A silence fell between the two men. It was broken when Uppard suddenly asked, 'How's Frank standing up to things?'

'Manion?'

'Who else!'

Adrian Slatter's expression became drawn. 'I curse the day I ever met him!'

'He's been a good client,' Uppard said in a taunting voice.

'He's a client this firm could have done without.'

'Frank's all right.'

'Frank's a ruthless criminal.'

'Ninety-eight per cent of our clients are criminals. Some one has to look after their interests.'

'I sometimes wish it didn't have to be me.'

'When will the trial finish?'

'Monday.'

'Did those papers I took along to Geddy's Chambers make any difference?'

'You didn't look through them by any chance?' Slatter enquired, and went on when Uppard shook his head, 'No, they didn't help in the slightest. I knew they wouldn't, but Frank was so insistent. Trouble is that he thinks he knows what's important and what isn't in a criminal trial.'

'What are his chances?'

'I've given up thinking about them.'

'He's not going to like it if he's sent down.'

'Let's hope he won't be,' Slatter said, almost as though it were a prayer to the deity who settled the fates of those standing in the Old Bailey dock.

Uppard shot him a look of surprise. One moment he was inveighing against this most potent of clients, the next expressing the quietly fervent hope that the jury would acquit him. Where exactly did his feelings lie?

Adrian Slatter turned his sluggish gaze to the clock on the mantelpiece. It was one which had been presented to his grandfather after forty years loyal service as accountant to a small firm of toy manufacturers. It was plain and ugly and though it did, at least, keep reasonably good time, it did little to mitigate the cheerless air of his office. But then nothing could overcome the depressing effect of the brown linoleum on the floor.

'I must get along to the Bailey. Frank always expects to see me before Court every morning. Where are you to-day?'

'Sessions.'

'Which?'

'Inner London.'

'Who?'

'Macken's up for trial.'

'I thought his money dried up and he was refused legal aid.'

Uppard grinned. 'It did, but he managed to find some and I took it off him before he blew it elsewhere.'

Adrian Slatter rose. 'See you this evening, George. Find out what you can about the Appleman case.'

'You, too, Mr Slatter, sir. You too!'

XI

Philip Quant lived alone in a small service flat in Chelsea. He had been there for three years since the break-up of his marriage and subsequent divorce. His wife had remarried – a solicitor this time – and now lived in the Midlands. There had been no children, so, from that point of view as well, the break had been clean and uncomplicated. Quant found that he missed very little after Rosemary departed and quickly reorganised his life so that the gap, such as it was, painlessly closed. She, for her part, so he gathered from third parties, was happy for the first time since she had gone up the aisle as a nervous bride of twenty.

On the morning after the Chambers meeting he had dressed, apart from his jacket, and was standing in the kitchen whistling tunelessly while he waited for the kettle to boil when the telephone rang. Turning down the gas, he went to answer it.

'It's Donald, sir. I've just had a call from Chief Superintendent Roffey and he'd like to see you.'

'But I saw him last night after the meeting.'

'I know, sir, but he wants to see you again.'

'What about?' Quant sounded displeased.

'I don't know, sir. He didn't say and I'm afraid I didn't ask him. I didn't feel it was my business . . .'

'No, all right, I don't suppose he'd have told you anyway. He's the sort of chap who loves sounding mysterious. What did you tell him?'

'I said that you weren't in Court to-day and that I thought you might be in Chambers later this morning, but I would let him know.'

'You've pretty well served me up to him on a plate,' Quant said crossly.

'I'm terribly sorry, sir. I can easily ring him and say that you're not available to-day . . .'

'And have him think all manner of dark things against me? No, I'll have to see him now.'

'I'm awfully sorry, sir, I didn't realise I'd be embarrassing you by telling him that.'

'That's all right, Donald, it's just that I don't like any police officer thinking I'm at his beck and call.'

'I'm sure Mr Roffey doesn't think that.'

'Hmm!'

'What do you want me to tell him, sir?'

'Say that I'll be in Chambers about half past ten and, though I have a lot of paper work to attend to, I'll see him then. And you can add that I hope he's not going to take up too much time.'

'I'll pass that on, sir.'

After Donald had rung off, Quant returned to the kitchen and made himself a mug of tea. He stood sipping it while gazing out of the window. There was nothing to look at except someone else's kitchen window, but his eyes saw nothing as his thoughts spread out like reconnoitring soldiers moving warily for fear of booby-traps.

He wished he had asked Donald whether he was the only person Roffey was wanting to see. He had half a mind to ring back and find out, but eventually decided against this as indicating anxiety about the interview. And he certainly didn't wish to give Donald that impression. Displeasure and annoyance were one thing, anxiety was something quite different.

He gave himself a second mug of tea and resumed his stance at the window. He still felt riled at what had happened.

He never had liked the police. He felt no obligation to assist them and he had no compunction about assailing their integrity when confronted by them as witnesses giving evidence against his clients.

To him, the policeman had never been a father-figure, but always someone who was ready to use his mite of authority to do you down.

It was scarcely surprising, having regard to his views and attitude, that he was no longer briefed on behalf of the police in any prosecution. It had not always been so, but dated from an occasion at the Old Bailey when in the course of defending a publican on a charge of handling stolen property he had suggested that the Yard's Assistant Commissioners were as susceptible to bribes, if large enough, as any other police officer. The suggestion had been received with icy contempt and Philip Quant's name had been struck off the list of those briefed on behalf of the Commissioner of Police of the Metropolis.

Though he realised he had overstepped the bounds not only of fact, but of propriety as well, his temperament prevented his making suitable amends and the ban had remained.

Having said that he would be in Chambers by half past ten, he timed his arrival for a quarter to eleven.

Roffey and Chisett were seated in the clerks' room waiting for him. Ignoring them completely he said to Donald, 'I'll let you know as soon as I'm ready.' He then disappeared into his own room.

Roffey continued to sit with a masklike expression after Quant had gone. He failed to register any reaction to what was an obviously calculated affront. One hand rested on the handle of his umbrella and the other lightly held his bowler hat which he had declined to hang on one of the pegs Donald had indicated. His posture was that of a Victorian gentleman about to be photographed.

'I'm sure he won't keep you long,' Donald said defensively as they heard Quant's door close behind him. 'He's just got one or two things to attend to and then he'll be free to see you.'

Roffey gave the briefest nod which managed to convey that he had heard, even if he did not accept, this vicariously proffered apology.

'Sheila not in to-day?' Chisett enquired suddenly.

Donald looked embarrassed. 'She'll be back shortly. Actually, she's gone out on an errand for me.'

The truth was, however, that as soon as she had heard that Roffey would be coming to Chambers, she had firmly stated she did not propose to come face to face with him and had gone off to the Old Bailey with some papers which Donald had to get there anyway.

'Quite recovered, has she?' Chisett went on.

'She seems all right to-day,' Donald said cautiously.

'I suppose *you've* met her young man?' Roffey asked, turning his head slowly in Donald's direction.

'Yes, not that I know him well.'

'Jealous type by all accounts,' Chisett said.

Donald shrugged and vaguely gestured inability to answer such a question. 'I really couldn't say.'

'He seemed pretty nervous when we saw him yesterday. He couldn't sit still and his eyes were darting all over the place. How long have he and Sheila known each other?'

'About a couple of years, I think.'

'Is that before or after Sheila came to Chambers?'

'I think she met him just before she joined us.'

'That's what she says. He, too, for that matter.' He observed Donald's expression. 'Only doing a bit of cross-checking,' he explained.

Roffey frowned slightly as though disapproving of his sergeant's questions.

There was a buzz on the switchboard and Donald plugged in a lead and put a headphone to one ear.

'Right, sir, I'll bring them along straight away,' he said. Turning to Roffey and Chisett, he added, 'Mr Quant's ready to see you now.'

Philip Quant was at his desk reading a brief when they entered. Without raising his head he said, 'Find yourselves chairs and sit down.'

He continued reading for several seconds before looking up.

'Yes, Superintendent,' he said in a tone of exaggerated long-suffering, 'what can I do for you to-day? I thought we were supposed to have covered everything last night. I can only assume that something fresh has cropped up, what is it?'

Roffey stared at him impassively for half a minute or more. He had pulled up a chair to one corner of Quant's desk and was sitting bolt upright.

Detective Sergeant Chisett had also pulled his chair up to a corner of the desk and was smoothing open his notebook.

'Would you care to tell me, sir, what your relationship with the dead man was?'

'I wasn't related to him at all.'

'I think you know I didn't mean that, sir. How did you get on with him?'

'How did I get on with him? I scarcely knew him. He wasn't my pupil and he'd been in Chambers only just over a couple of months.'

'Did you like him?'

Quant frowned. Roffey's tone, more than the actual questions, was disconcerting. It was as though he was prepared to put up with insult or evasion, knowing that he held all the trump cards and couldn't lose in the end.

'I neither liked nor disliked him.'

'No?'

'Look, Superintendent, I don't know what you're getting at, but I suggest we're both too old to play word games with each other.'

'I'm delighted to hear you say that, Mr Quant. Did you ever have a row with Appleman?'

'What sort of a row?'

'Any sort of a row?'

'No, of course I didn't,' Quant said testily. 'Why on earth should I have rows with someone else's pupil?'

'Make a note, Sergeant, that Mr Quant says he never had a row with the deceased,' Roffey said in a *deus ex machina* voice.

Philip Quant bit his lip angrily.

'I rather resent the way you're conducting this interview. If you wish it to continue, perhaps you'd stop treating me like one of the moronic criminals you're probably more used to questioning.'

'If you don't wish to co-operate, sir, you only have to say so.'

For a moment it looked as though Quant was about to lose his temper. But in the end, he said, 'Go ahead, get on with it.'

'Are you sure there wasn't some hostility between you?'

'I presume that you must be satisfied there was or you wouldn't keep on pressing this line of question. It might be better if you disclosed your source of information. I can only think that you have been listening to some backstair gossip.'

'The deceased kept a diary,' Roffey said, fixing his gaze intently on Quant's face. The simple statement of fact appeared to hit him right between the eyes. He looked stunned for a second or two, then his face flushed with colour. When he spoke, his voice sounded unnaturally taut.

'And there's some reference to me in this diary?'

'Yes.'

'Am I to be told what?'

'He refers to having a row with you and says you obviously didn't like him.'

'Is that all?'

'Yes.'

'He didn't say what this supposed row was about?'

'Not in so many words.' It was Roffey's turn to sound slightly on the defensive.

'I see.' Quant stared thoughtfully at the wall while the two officers watched him from either end of the desk. Slowly he returned his attention to Roffey. 'We might have avoided all this shadow-boxing if you'd told me about the diary in the first place. I think I know what Appleman must have been referring to and it tends to confirm my view of him.' He paused and assumed a judicial air. 'I suppose it was about two or three weeks ago, he approached me one evening and asked me what I thought his chances were of staying on in Chambers as a tenant when his pupillage with

James Geddy was over. Quite frankly I was a bit embarrassed and I told him it was far too early to canvass his prospects, that it would depend on whether there were any vacancies when the time arrived and on the impression he had created. And as to that, I said that Geddy and Donald were the two people who'd best be able to assess his ability and prospects. I remember mentioning in a semi-serious way that Donald was the most important person in Chambers to impress. That young barristers depended on the clerk, more than anyone else, to get them work and this would only happen if he considered them suitable.' His brow contracted in a frown. 'However, to my surprise and, indeed, further embarrassment, he continued to press the question of his staying on in Chambers and in the end I was rather sharp with him. I told him, in effect, that he was being importunate and was going about things in the worst possible way if that was what he really did want. Despite that he tried to argue with me and suggested I might pull strings for him, so that finally I was forced to be extremely rude to him. He then became very huffy and we eventually parted on somewhat strained terms.' He glanced at Chisett and back to Roffey. 'That, I imagine is the row referred to in his diary.'

'Where did this take place?' Roffey asked.

'In this room.'

'What was the follow-up?'

'If you mean what was the aftermath, the answer is that Appleman rather went out of his way to avoid me and I was at pains to behave as though nothing had happened.'

'You said just now that the incident you've described tended to confirm your view of the deceased. Can you explain what you meant?'

Quant delicately fingered his chin as his expression became self-important.

'It's difficult to explain without sounding snobbish,' he said, 'but quite frankly I thought he was a bit too obviously on the make. In fact as anyone'll tell you, I'm the least snobbish of people, but Appleman always struck me as a go-getter of the less attractive type. It was as though he was unwilling to learn the ways of the Bar, but was determined to bulldoze his way into the profession.' His mouth twisted into a deprecating smile. 'If you can't be well-bred, at least you can be sensitive. He was neither.'

Quant leaned back in his chair and ran a hand through his lank fair hair which fell across his head from a long parting rather like a horse's mane. The face was pale, the eyes restless and the mouth looked secretly amused and petulant by turns.

All this Roffey took in as he stared at him. He was sure that Quant had not told him the truth – or certainly not as much of the truth as lay within his knowledge. And for someone of the professional standing of a barrister to with-hold the truth was, in Roffey's view, highly significant. That Quant was not a man of the highest integrity was already apparent from the blemish in his past. The leopard did not change his spots etcetera ... If you could embrace deception once in the cause of dishonesty, you could do so again to conceal your moral failings. Though murder was, perhaps, rather more than a moral failing. But the principle remained.

The more he thought about it, the more dissatisfied he felt with the way the interview had gone. Once he had disclosed that the diary entry referred only to a row without stating what it was about, he had handed the initiative to Quant who had not missed the opportunity of exploiting it. On the other hand, he didn't really see how he could have avoided the position and it might yet prove to have its advantage. That is if he could show that Quant had deliber-ately lied to him.

The really significant thing was that he had been given a picture of the deceased which was completely at variance with the others he had received. Everyone else had spoken well of Robin Appleman. Admittedly he had his faults, but he seemed a generally likeable person. And that was the view of everyone from the head of Chambers to the clerk. Of everyone, save Philip Quant. But was it simply that

Quant spoke frankly where others mouthed cocktail party politenesses? The A.C. had warned him that the ranks would be closed against him, with the suggestion that they might go through the motions of helping him but would resist any serious attempt to probe more deeply than they were prepared to have happen.

Roffey decided that he would have to suspend judgment for the time being. But Quant still remained the man in his sights. This was the angle on which he must concentrate. Perhaps Quant's own pupil might prove to be a source of information. He must tackle him again, though with velvet gloves. He didn't doubt his capacity to do this. However he might appear to the world at large, he knew he was a versatile interrogator who could, when occasion arose, adopt any number of different ploys in conducting an interview.

He was aware of Quant's voice breaking in on his thoughts.

'If that's all, Superintendent, I have some work to get on with.'

Roffey rose and went across to retrieve his hat and umbrella – he wore a topcoat only in the very coldest weather, a dark blue one with a black velvet collar. Chisett also got up, slipping his notebook into his pocket. He had left his rumpled raincoat and wide-brimmed brown hat in a heap on the floor of the clerk's room.

'Yes, that's certainly all for the time being, Mr Quant, though I may well want to see you again.'

Quant frowned. Roffey seemed altogether too pleased with himself for a public servant who had just been accorded an audience by a busy member of the Bar and put fairly firmly in his place.

'You can show yourselves out can't you?' he said, making no effort to leave his chair.

'Behaves like some medieval duke,' Chisett muttered as he closed the door behind them.

Lowering his voice, Roffey said, 'We're going to find out everything we can about him. *Everything.*'

'You think he may have done it?' Chisett asked with

lively interest.

'I think precisely that,' Roffey said and stalked off towards the clerks' room.

Donald met them at the door.

'Everything all right?' he enquired hopefully rather in the manner of an anxious *maître d'hôtel*.

Roffey ignored the question and peered past him into the room where Sheila was on the telephone.

'I can't talk to you any longer,' she was saying. 'I'll call you back as soon as they've gone.'

She put down the receiver, turned round and gave a small gasp as she saw the two officers standing outside the door with Donald rather obviously blocking the entrance.

'Good morning, Miss Hamer,' Roffey said. 'Would that have been Mr Dixon you were speaking to on the phone?' Sheila glowered. 'Don't tell me if you don't want to.'

'Yes, it was,' she replied, resentfully.

'I only asked as I may want to see him again later today.'

Let her pass that on, Roffey thought with relish.

There were some witnesses from whom you concealed your intention of seeking an interview : others to whom you advertised it in advance. Roffey judged Alan Dixon to fall into the latter category. The more he was kept on tenterhooks the better; the more the tension was stoked up, the greater likelihood of his cracking – if he had anything to crack over. Sergeant Chisett certainly thought he had and though Roffey's nature did not permit him to acknowledge publicly any merit in the theories of his underlings, he never privately disregarded them.

Donald accompanied them across the lobby to the door.

'I don't imagine we've seen the last of you, Mr Roffey,' he said in an attempt at joviality as he held the door open.

'I expect we'll be back.' Roffey's tone was non-committal.

'Are you pleased with progress so far?' Donald asked,

knowing that everyone in Chambers expected him to keep both ears to the ground.

Roffey looked at him thoughtfully.

'You'd be surprised how often in a murder enquiry, people find reasons for not coming out with the whole truth. But you must have come across it yourself in the cases handled by your barristers.'

Donald nodded, a rather sickly smile fixed on his face.

'Let me now ask you a question,' Roffey went on, leaning relaxedly on his umbrella. 'Why did Mr Quant dislike the deceased so much?'

Donald licked his lips. 'But Mr Appleman wasn't Mr Quant's pupil!'

'Quite true, but would you still care to answer my question?'

'I had no idea Mr Quant did dislike him. I'm sure he had no reason to . . . Their paths wouldn't cross all that often . . .'

'But he did. Very much!'

'Perhaps you ought to ask Mr Quant.'

'Oh, I have and he's given me a reason. I just wanted to hear what you'd say.'

'I'm afraid I can't help you.'

Roffey straightened up, tipped his umbrella in farewell and turned on his heel. Chisett followed him, hat clamped on the back of his head and raincoat in a ball under his arm.

For several seconds, Donald remained standing in the doorway, as though mesmerised by their retreating backs.

He felt bewildered, anxious and distinctly frightened. What was happening to Chambers? It was as though all the furies had suddenly decided that their corporate life was too easy and too secure and must be subjected to a demoniacally destructive assault.

XII

Almost everyone in Number 1 Court at the Old Bailey was glad that it was Friday and that the weekend was no more than a few hours away. Reasons differed, but relief at the thought was universal.

The judge, improbably from his rather parchment appearance, was looking forward to getting into his small workshop where he was presently engaged in making a model diesel-electric locomotive, complete to the last detail, for one of his grandsons. Using his hands at a lathe, alone and uninterrupted, was a blessed relief after a week in Court. It was like sailing single-handed round the world after a decade of enduring the relentless pressures of urban life.

Peter Strange, who led for the prosecution, could hardly wait to be out on the golf course. Winter, summer, rain or shine, this was where he spent his weekends, or as much of them as he could decently wrest from his family.

James Geddy was normally content to let the weekends come and go and to leave their organisation to his wife. More often than not he had to take work home which had to be fitted in at some stage, but this consideration apart, he welcomed someone else making the decisions and generally fell in with whatever was suggested. But he found himself viewing this coming weekend quite differently. Instead of regarding it, as he usually did, as chocolate soufflé after a week of bread and butter pudding (he liked both), he saw its approach as a haven from storm-whipped seas. He felt that the last twenty-four hours had added as many years to his age. Robin's death had shattered him and he could hardly bring himself to realise that it was only the previous day the appalling discovery had been made. It had spun him right off his axis, so that, whatever the outcome, he felt nothing could be the same again. It was a sensation which frightened him and one for which he was quite unprepared. He had reached an age and acquired an experience of life which he had cosily imagined would immunise him against the more severe effects of shock. But it was not so and it was only by exerting enormous self-control that he had been able to continue with the Manion case.

Part of his mind told him that the weekend might well bring no relief, might perhaps exacerbate his state of restless strain as there would be no compulsion for his thoughts to dwell elsewhere, but he still looked forward to it with a fevered avidity. Anything to get away from Number 1 Court, from Slatter, from Manion and from every association with his pupil's death. Such is the perversity of human nature that he might long to return on Monday to that familiar scene, however sour it now appeared to be. He recognised this possibility, but, for the moment, he knew that all he wanted was to be away from it – for ever.

With luck he would finish his final speech to the jury this afternoon which would leave him only with a plea in mitigation to make on Monday in the event of Manion being convicted. And, as everyone in the profession knew, making a plea in mitigation for a man such as Frank Manion was like spitting into a gale. But it would be expected of him and the judge would probably go through the well-worn ritual of thanking him and of informing the prisoner that, but for the mitigating factors so cogently and persuasively advanced by his counsel, he would have received a far longer sentence than that about to be passed. Except, being old Tyler, he probably would not waste time on such clichés. Anyway, what did it matter, he would never see Manion again and the completion of the case would see the end of the fare. Barristers like cabbies wait in the rank to be hired. The journey over, they pick up the next client or passenger.

He sat back and closed his eyes. Strange had just begun his final speech to the jury. As long as he listened with one ear, he could afford to let his thoughts go elsewhere. Not that the choice was other than pre-determined. Suddenly his feeling of blind despair gave way to one of rising anger. How dare anyone not merely commit such a dastardly murder, but involve him so casually in its commission! All right, so it was a selfish way of looking at it, but he had a right to view it selfishly and it didn't in any way detract from the sorrow he felt about Robin's death. But involved he most certainly was and heaven alone knew to what further extent the involvement might increase – or with what consequences to his life, both professional and private.

It was while his thoughts were running along these lines, that he felt a slight tap on his shoulder and turned to find that David was trying to hand him a folded note. It read:

'Holly and I are going down to Somerset this weekend and thought we'd drop in on Robin's parents to see if there was anything we could do. Is there anything you would like us to do or say?'

James Geddy picked up his pen and wrote at the bottom:

'We'll have a word later.'

In writing the note, David had thought it better not to say specifically that a visit to Robin's home was the prime object of their journey, as Geddy might have probed their reasons and subsequently have expressed disapproval. David was pretty sure that he would not approve any amateur sleuthing and, as a senior member of Chambers with Chambers very much involved, it would have been difficult to have gone against his advice.

As it was, David was exhilarated by the prospect. He had always been a young man of swift decision and action, sometimes with disastrous results but more often with success and a sense of personal satisfaction. First decisions are usually the right ones, but not always so and it remained to be seen, he realised, how well his temperament fitted him for the Bar. At least he was enjoying his first taste of the life, and that seemed to be the main thing, although he deplored the sometimes seemingly endless spinning-out of a trial. The lists were clogged with prisoners awaiting trial, the delays became longer every year and yet judge and counsel gave the impression of having the rest of their lives to spend on any case. Perhaps when *he* was being paid by the day, he would also share this relish for 'lentissimo' in a criminal trial. On one occasion he had actually timed the silences in the course of a single hour and they had added up to thirteen and a half minutes, though it was fair to say that this had been largely accounted for by a notoriously slow judge who insisted upon personally recording every spoken word and whose writing was as painfully slow as the workings of his mind.

Like James Geddy, Adrian Slatter longed for the weekend simply to get away from Number 1 Court and his demanding client who occupied its centrepiece. He knew exactly how he was going to spend it in his endeavour to forget the strains of the past few days. He was going out on a blind. Alcohol and sex were the chosen instruments of suppression. Not too much of the one, or he wouldn't be able to enjoy the other, but if he could judge the quantities aright amnesia should be complete. As he sat at the table in front of James Geddy with his lowered head resting on his hands, he licked his lips in anticipation.

Not very estimable, perhaps, but having clients like Manion didn't help one's self-esteem anyway.

He glanced wearily at his watch. It was half past twelve. The morning was almost over and with luck the judge would rise early this afternoon seeing that it was Friday. He hoped so. He could hardly wait to be freed from the atmosphere the trial had taken on and to hurry away on his mission of forgetting. He gave a small shiver as he reflected that the weekend must, however, come to an end. But at this moment he was not prepared to look any farther ahead.

Sitting in the commanding position of the dock of Number 1 Court, Frank Manion glanced down at his counsel and solicitor. At first he felt a spurt of anger when he realised that the trial wouldn't finish that day, but now he thought there might be some advantage even though it meant a further dreary weekend in Brixton prison. Speeches should finish and the judge might well have begun his summing-up which would provide an inkling of the verdict he was after. If it did reach that stage, it would give him an opportunity of weighing his own options . . .

It was at about this moment that Detective Chief Superintendent Roffey slipped into Court and took an unobserved seat at the back, cocking his head on one side to tune in immediately on what was happening.

'Members of the jury,' Strange was saying, 'it would be unrealistic of me not to mention a tragic event which has cast its shadow across this trial and, in particular, over those of us who sit on counsels' benches. I refer, of course, to the sudden death of Mr Appleman who had his place behind my learned friend until yesterday. As I say, members of the jury, it would be unrealistic not to mention it when you and all of us taking part in this trial have been made so much aware of it by the quickening of interest not so much in this trial as in us, its participants. And yet, as I am sure you will be aware, this tragic and horrible event has no relevance whatsoever to your considerations. Your concern is purely with evidence, with what the witnesses have told you under oath in relation to the issues you are trying. You will not, I know, allow outside events to affect your judgment or to distract you from what properly are your duties as jurors in this case . . .'

Roffey glanced around. The Court was packed. Manion's trial had attracted maximum attention from the outset, but there was no doubt that Robin Appleman's murder had invested the proceedings with additional drama. People crowded into Court to identify in some strange mystical way with what had happened. Violent death has always cast its morbid and hypnotic spell. People stand and stare in absolute stillness, their senses sharp and quivering like well-trained pointer dogs.

'Members of the jury,' Strange went on, 'what it comes down to is whether you accept the inferences to be drawn from the prosecution's evidence or whether you accept the unsupported – and, the crown suggests, glibly implausible – explanation of the accused. I ask you to say that the facts which the prosecution have proved in evidence give rise to inescapable inferences as to the Criminal intentions of the accused and that his attempts in the course of his own evidence to coat his conduct with a gloss of innocence were transparent and unbelievable. You will recall that at one point when he was being examined-in-chief by my learned friend, he mentioned that there was some document or documents in existence which would show he had honest intentions and rebut the inference of criminal deception.

'Well, members of the jury, you have probably waited, as I have, to see this important material. We have waited in vain, have we not! The moment for its appearance has passed and no further mention has been made of it. What inference do you draw from that, members of the jury? That no such documents exist which would prove the accused's innocence in this transaction? What other explanation can there be for their non-appearance? It's entirely a matter for you but surely that inference *is* irresistible . . .'

Roffey looked across at Manion who was staring at prosecuting counsel with an expression of quiet malevolence.

A few minutes later, the judge enquired of Strange how much longer he was likely to be. On being told at least another quarter of an hour, he pursed his lips, stared at the clock and then announced that the Court would adjourn until two o'clock. Just before rising, he looked towards James Geddy and said:

'Mr Geddy, I wish neither to embarrass nor inhibit you, least of all do I wish to tie you down, but it might assist me if you were able to give me some idea of how long you expect to be addressing the jury? But please don't answer if it doesn't suit you to do so.'

'My lord, I'm neither embarrassed nor inhibited and I'm grateful for knowing that any estimate I give your lordship is not expected to be of binding effect. I would think about an hour, my lord. I cannot believe I shall be longer than that.'

'Thank you, Mr Geddy,' Mr Justice Tyler said.

As James Geddy and David made their way out of Court Roffey stepped forward.

'I wonder if I might have a brief word with you, Mr Geddy. I won't keep you long, but it's something I'd like to clear up as soon as possible.'

'Very well.' Geddy's tone was edgy. 'If we hang on here for half a minute, the Court'll be empty and it'll be the quietest spot we'll find.'

'It's only this,' Roffey said as they stood by the door after the last person had gone, 'did Mr Appleman ever speak to you about staying on in your Chambers after he had completed his pupillage?'

James Geddy looked surprised. 'No, the subject was never raised. Apart from anything else, it would have been premature anyway.'

'He never dropped any hints about it?'

'Never.'

'Supposing he had, what would have been your reaction?'

'I'd have told him it was too soon to start thinking about it.'

'Do you think he did stand a chance of becoming a permanent member of Chambers?'

'I've no idea. He hadn't yet stood on his feet in Court. As you may know, pupils are not allowed to during the first six months of their pupillage. It's a Bar Council ruling of several years back.'

Roffey nodded in an abstracted way. 'As far as you're concerned then, Mr Geddy, he never pushed himself or openly tried to win your vote or however it's done?'

'Certainly not. I've no doubt he hoped to become a tenant – most pupils do – but he never canvassed his prospects with me.'

'And you'd have been the most likely person if he had wanted to raise the matter?'

Geddy frowned. 'I imagine so. May I ask the reason for your questions? They're presumably based on something you've heard?'

'It's just the endless process of checks and cross-checks,' Roffey said with a small smile. 'I don't think I'd better say more at this stage and I mustn't keep you any longer from your lunch.'

Roffey opened the door. 'I wonder if Mr March is still around? It might be a convenient moment to have a further word with him.'

David had been in two minds whether to wait for Geddy and had eventually decided to do so. He was talking to Adrian Slatter when the two men emerged from Court. Slatter looked expectantly at Roffey who gave him a brief nod.

'I'd like to have a word with you, Mr March, if you can spare a moment. I shan't keep you long.'

David blushed. Had his and Holly's invasion of Robin's flat been discovered?

'Oh, sure,' he said uncomfortably.

'Do you want to see me, too?' Slatter enquired.

'Not at the moment, Mr Slatter,' Roffey replied in the tone of a schoolmaster releasing an errant pupil.

The corridor outside Number 1 Court was now empty and Roffey led the way to a deserted alcove.

'Did Mr Appleman ever discuss with you his chances of staying on in Chambers as a permanent ... I believe "tenant" is the word, isn't it?'

'I imagine it's always a topic among pupils,' David said, with a silent sigh of relief that the interview was not on the subject he had been fearing. 'We certainly talked about it among ourselves from time to time. That's to say, Robin, Holly Childersley, and myself.'

'Did he hope to stay on?'

'We all did. They're good Chambers and good Chambers are not easy to come by.'

'Do you know whether he discussed his prospects with anyone else in Chambers?'

David looked puzzled. 'I've no idea. I suppose he might have had a word on the side with Donald, but he never mentioned it.'

'You're Mr Quant's pupil?' Roffey said thoughtfully after a short silence.

'Yes.'

'I would ask you, Mr March, to treat what I'm about to say in strictest confidence. The reason will be obvious. It's about Mr Quant.'

David experienced a frisson of apprehension, but gave a nod to show that he accepted the position.

'What sort of a man is he?' Roffey asked.

'He's a good lawyer and he's a good pupil-master and he's always been very nice to me.'

'How does he get on with his contemporaries in Chambers? With Mr Geddy, for example?'

David bit his lower lip. 'It's a bit embarrassing for me to answer that sort of question.'

'I understand that, but I'm sure you wish to have your friend's murder solved.' After a pause he added, 'Not that I'm suggesting Mr Quant is a murderer, though there are one or two things about him which puzzle me. And I believe you can probably help me.'

Choosing his words with considerable care, David said, 'I don't think there's the same rapport between Mr Quant and the others of his seniority as there is between themselves. I don't mean that they quarrel or don't get on with him, but he's the odd man out in some ways. He can sometimes behave a bit childishly. Well, not childish childishly so much as petulantly and even perhaps irresponsibly. He's a bit of a gossipmonger and is, I suspect, not above stirring up a mite of trouble just for his own amusement.'

'That's a very helpful picture of him,' Roffey observed. 'And, if I may say so, an obviously carefully painted one.'

'I hope so,' David said uncertainly, 'because personally I get on well with him and, as I say, he's been very good to me. I would hate to say anything unfair, but, if this really may be important to your investigation, I should attempt to be as truthful as I can.'

'Exactly. And you can rest assured that I shall respect your confidence. Do you know what Mr Quant thought of Mr Appleman?'

David started as though the question had drilled a nerve.

'I don't think he liked him,' he said slowly.

'Why not?'

'I've no idea.' He looked straight into Roffey's eyes. 'I really haven't any idea. It was only the night of Robin's death that I first had an inkling. Philip Quant and I were going up to the Templar for a drink and Philip was trying to persuade Robin to come too, though it was obvious that he didn't want to, and when he absolutely refused to join us, Philip made some derogatory comments about him. It wasn't so much what he said as the way he spoke which showed his feelings.'

'And that was the first indication you had of his dislike?'

'Yes.'

'Did it surprise you?'

'Very much.'

'I expect you've thought about it since?'

'Yes, I have.'

'With any result?'

'Absolutely none. I'm baffled. I can't think what can have arisen between them. They virtually never saw each other except over a beer at the Templar when we were all there together or in a roomful of people in Chambers.'

'There must be an explanation,' Roffey persisted. 'Dislike of that sort has to have some basis.'

'I know, but I've no idea what it was in this case.'

A silence fell as Roffey wondered whether to put Quant's own explanation to David for his reaction and decided against. At the same time, David was wondering whether to tell Roffey of the letter he and Holly had found at Robin's flat, but concluded that to do so might create more difficulties than otherwise. Anyway, it was bound sooner or later to come into police hands. Simliarly there was no point in mentioning the proposed visit to Robin's home, which might only arouse suspicion – and quite unnecessarily so.

'I'm very grateful to you, Mr March. Our little chat has been most useful. I hope there's still time for you to get some lunch.'

Roffey adjusted his bowler, unhooked his umbrella off his arm and, waving it in farewell salute, strode off. His step was more confident and determined than usual.

XIII

David picked up Holly at eight o'clock the next morning and they completed the 145 miles journey in just under four hours. The T.R.6 didn't get many opportunities of a long run these days and it seemed to enjoy the open stretches of road after the fits and starts of London use. David enjoyed driving, that is he enjoyed the conscious co-ordination of mind and limb in order to get the best out of his car. He was dressed in a sports jacket and pair of slacks and had at the last moment remembered that he ought to wear a black tie. This went rather incongruously with his bold check shirt, but by then it was too late to change and, anyway, it was not as though he was going to be chief mourner at an Irish funeral. He suspected, however, that Robin's parents would be the type to observe the niceties of every situation. Robin had obviously been brought up strictly and David guessed that the bounds of the so-called permissive society stopped short of his home.

Holly was wearing a black woollen trouser suit and her hair was tied back in a red ribbon. She explained to David that the suit was new and had not been bought with any thought of mourning in mind.

As they entered the outskirts of Taunton, David drew up beside a policeman and asked the way.

The policeman, an earnest young man, gave them some

complicated directions which he repeated twice and they set off again.

It required two further requests for help and a number of wrong turns before they reached their destination.

'This is it!' David said as they both peered out of the car at the figures 62 painted in black on the glass panel above the front door.

It was the right-hand half of a semi-detached built around the early thirties. A short paved path led from the newly painted blue gate to the door. There was a small square of lawn with a pillar rose growing in a centre bed and a further bed in front of the bay window on the right of the front door. It all managed to look neat and tidy and well cared for even in mid-November.

Lace curtains across the lower halves of all the windows hid what movement there might be behind.

Holly and Robin got out and walked self-consciously up to the front door. Holly pressed the bell, which they could hear ring inside. Almost immediately footsteps approached and the door was opened to reveal a short, plump woman with grey hair, wearing an enveloping floral pinafore.

'Mrs Appleman?' David said. She nodded. 'Mrs Appleman, this is Holly Childersley and I'm David March. We were fellow-pupils of Robin's at 4 Mulberry Court. We happened to be near here and felt we should like to drop in and express our deepest sympathy over this terrible thing that's happened.'

Mrs Appleman's eyes had never left David's face while he had been speaking, but now she said, 'Please come in.'

She led the way into the front room which had a cold, unused air. She bent down and lit the gas-fire.

'I hope you'll be warm enough in here. Won't you sit down.'

When they were seated, she perched herself on the edge of a chair and looked at them.

'We wanted you to know,' Holly, said breaking an uncomfortable silence, 'how much we liked Robin and how dreadful we all feel about his death. I know it's nothing to how you and Mr Appleman must be feeling and it's hard to put things into words, but . . .'

'I'm afraid Mr Appleman's out,' she said, as though seizing on the only thing Holly had mentioned which she felt able to comment on. 'And Rosemary is, too. She's my daughter.'

'Yes, I remember Robin used to mention her.'

'Robin hadn't been home for several weeks, but he hoped to come for a weekend soon. I expect he was working too hard.'

'He was getting on very well,' David said eagerly.

Mrs Appleman nodded. 'He'd always set his heart on becoming a barrister, though it's not really our line at all. My folk are all farmers and my husband's father and grandfather worked on the railway.' She gazed into the red glow of the fire. 'There's too much wickedness in the world these days, especially in big cities like London. All this violence.'

Holly and David nodded gravely. They were both considerably relieved to find her so composed. Composed to the point of being almost withdrawn from the reality of what had happened.

'Would you like a cup of tea?' she asked, looking quickly from one to the other. 'Or I can offer you a glass of cider.'

'I'd love some cider,' Holly said, while David nodded.

When Mrs Appleman had gone out of the room, David said, 'Do you think we can steer the conversation round?'

'Yes.'

A minute later, Mrs Appleman returned with two glasses of cider on a tray.

'I gather that even though you didn't see Robin very often, he kept in regular touch with you by letter. He was always writing them in free moments.'

'Yes, he was a good writer.'

'So you knew all about the sort of life we lead as pupils?'

'Oh yes. He's mentioned both of you in conversation and letters.'

'We all three got on very well together,' David said, glancing at Holly for confirmation. She nodded. 'Have you ever met Mr Geddy, his pupil-master?'

'No, but Robin used to speak well of him and I had a nice letter from him this morning. He sounds a nice man.'

'He is. Very.'

'There was someone, though, he didn't like,' Mrs Appleman remarked suddenly.

David raised his eyebrows. 'In Chambers, do you mean?' he asked in a faintly incredulous tone.

'Yes, it was in his last letter, he said he'd had a row with this person.'

'I wonder who it can have been,' David said, looking at Holly with an expression of well-simulated surprise.

'Robin mentioned his name, but we couldn't read his writing. The more he studied, the worse his writing got,' she added.

'Do you still have this letter?' David enquired in what he hoped sounded a casual tone.

But the question was scarcely out before she shook her head. 'No, I don't keep letters. Not even his. There's enough clutter about a house without adding to it by bits of paper. Once I'd replied, I'd throw his letters away.'

A glance round the room in which they were sitting was enough to confirm what Mrs Appleman said. It was tidy to the point of discomfort. Nothing was out of place and David felt that if he leaned forward for a second, she would dart to plump up the cushion behind him or dash away for a dustpan and brush should any dirt come away from his shoes. She had pointedly put out two small mats for their glasses after she had handed the cider to them.

'I wonder who on earth it can have been, David?' Holly said, as it were striking the gong a second time.

'It was a short name,' Mrs Appleman said.

'It surely couldn't have been Donald, the clerk,' David remarked with a frown.

'Who else is there?' Holly added. 'A short name! Not Mr Ainsworth or Miss Rayner ...'

'My name's short,' David put in, 'but I've never had a row with Robin.'

Oh God, this is awful, he thought, perhaps it would be better to call it a day. The last thing Robin and I ever did together was have words, even though I know I'm not the person referred to in the letter. How I'm beginning to hate this, he reflected with a sudden feeling of self-loathing.

'Could it have been Mr Quant he was referring to?' Holly went on.

'How do you spell that?' Mrs Appleman asked.

'Q-U-A-N-T.'

'It could have been something like that. Anyway, I wrote back and told him to avoid having rows with people. They don't help anyone. But Robin was always a bit excitable from when he was a little boy. He'd get upset easily.' Her expression softened suddenly. 'He was such a pretty little boy . . .'

It seemed that they had learnt all they had hoped to find out and that the time had come to retire as decently as they could.

'I think most people in Chambers would like to come to the funeral when it's arranged, Mrs Appleman,' David said, moving as though to get up from his chair.

'I don't know when it'll be,' she said. 'It depends on the police.' Her tone was bleak and forlorn.

'Have the police been to see you?'

'Yes. The local police, they get messages from London and come and ask us questions, not that there's anything we can tell them. What do we know?'

'Mrs Appleman, I should have said this before, but Mr Geddy asked me particularly to tell you that you weren't to hesitate to get in touch with him and if there's anything he can do to help you.'

She nodded her head slowly. 'I don't see there's much anyone can do. Robin's gone and nothing'll bring him back.'

She accompanied them to the front door, thanked them politely but briefly for coming and closed the door before they had reached the gate.

'Shall we go straight back to town?' David asked.

'Yes, unless you want to . . .'

'I'd sooner drive straight back,' David broke in firmly.

They did not speak again until they were out in the open country. Then Holly said:

'It's only just occurred to me that she never once asked me anything about who might have killed Robin. I suppose in a curious way she's not interested. He's dead and that's all she's concerned with. She assumes it was some outsider who'll be eventually caught and dealt with, but she's content to let others cope with that problem.'

'It'll probably be something like that,' David agreed. 'She seemed a quiet, self-contained sort of person. One who'd very much mind her own business and avoid crossing other people's paths.' He did a quick change-down and accelerated past a heavy lorry whose exhaust fumes were beginning to become obnoxious. 'It was obviously Philip with whom Robin had this row,' he said after he had regained his own side of the road.

'Yes, but what on earth could it have been about?'

'The whole thing's a mystery,' David remarked in a slowly thoughtful tone.

They stopped once on the way back and had a cup of coffee but it was soon after five o'clock when they pulled up outside Holly's flat.

It had been a strange day and one which had turned out differently from David's expectations. Except that on reflection he realised that it was not so much the happenings of the day as his reaction to them which differed from what he had expected.

Among other things, they had served to draw him closer to Holly so that he took it for granted they would spend the evening together.

It was several hours later as they lay half-undressed on top of her bed that he reflected again what a strange day it had been.

Holly for her part had fallen quietly asleep, her head snuggled against his side. She looked small and vulnerable and very unbarristerial.

139

He smiled wryly in the darkened room. It should be the other way round, he thought. It's the male who is always supposed to sink into indecorous slumber.

XIV

George Uppard paced up and down the lawyers' interview room at Brixton Prison. It was a cheerless place to be on a Saturday afternoon and far removed from Uppard's usual spot on the terrace of a football ground. But the message he had received had managed to impart a note of urgency though its actual wording had been no more dramatic than: 'I want to see you to-day. Don't tell Slatter. Frank.'

It had been brought by hand by a youth who did a paper-round in the area and who was ready, for a price, to deliver notes which could be easily enough smuggled out of the prison. As London's chief remand prison, Brixton's daily arrivals and departures rivalled those of a transit camp.

A door opened and Manion came in escorted by a prison officer who sat down at a discreet distance, pulled a dog-eared paperback from his hip pocket and buried himself in it.

'Hello, Frank. Got your message. Came right away.'

Manion smiled. It was a smile of personal satisfaction rather than a greeting to his visitor.

'Thought you would,' he said, adding quickly, 'You've not told Slatter?'

'No.'

'Good.'

There was a silence, during which Manion just stared at his visitor with a pensive expression.

'How's the trial going, Frank?' Uppard asked, rather as he might have enquired after a friend's holiday or mother-in-law.

'I've been let down. Let down bad.'

'How can you say that, Frank! You'll be a free man by Monday. The jury'll never convict on the tripey evidence the prosecution have brought.'

'I've still been let down,' Manion said baldly.

Uppard shook his head sorrowfully.

'Geddy's a good counsel. I'm sure he's done the case as well as anyone could.'

'Geddy's all right even if he looks a cold-hearted bastard, but I'm not talking about him. I'm talking about Slatter.'

'Slatter?'

'That's right, your boss, Slatter.'

'What's he supposed to have done?' Uppard asked warily.

Manion glanced quickly at the escort officer who still appeared to be absorbed in his book. Then leaning forward he said in a lowered voice, 'It's not what he's done, it's what he's not done. Now you listen to me carefully, George, because I'm not going to be mucked about any more. I need your help and if you wonder why you should give it, I'll tell you. And when I've told you, I don't think you'll need any further persuading.'

'Go ahead,' Uppard said in a studied tone, 'I'm listening.'

XV

Alan Dixon and Sheila had fallen into a Saturday routine from which departure was only possible at the risk of Alan going into a fit of aggressive sulks.

They would meet about midday, have an early light lunch at some relatively cheap café, then spend the afternoon in the cinema or wandering around the shops. About five o'clock they would return to Sheila's house which was empty, her parents following their own routine of visiting Sheila's mother's parents at Bromley.

They would then make love and around seven o'clock go out for the evening to dine and dance at one of the less pricy discotheques.

There were several things about the routine which Sheila didn't care for, chief among them the almost ritualistic early evening love-making. For her the hour was wrong and habit had made it more so.

She also felt they set off much too early for the last part of the day's events and she hated sitting in a virtually empty discotheque waiting for others to arrive and create the required atmosphere of pulsating humanity.

Admittedly they usually spent the best part of an hour in some pub on their way, but they still always arrived far too early.

But as she now knew very well, Alan was not an easy person to handle. A wrong word or gesture could cast a blight over a whole evening. For all that, his company excited her as no other man's had and his tempestuous nature provided her with a challenge she was prepared to meet certainly nine-tenths of the time.

On this particular Saturday, he was nervous and restless, and his love-making was almost frightening in its feverish intensity.

Afterwards, as he lay on his back smoking a cigarette and staring at the ceiling, he said, 'Do you think everything's going to be all right, Sheil?'

When he dropped the final 'a' from her name, it was a sign he was feeling vulnerable, that the anxious small boy in him had taken over.

Sheila, who was sitting on the edge of the bed idly rubbing a leg, turned and looked at him. 'Of course it is. What can go wrong?'

'The truth coming out.'

'It won't. It can't. Not unless one of us talks.'

'I wish it was all over now. I can't settle to anything. Every time I see a policeman, my heart comes up into my mouth.'

'You ought to come into Chambers and then you'd get

used to it. Roffey's always popping in and out. Incidentally, love, it'd be better if you didn't phone me there for the time being.'

Alan looked at her anxiously. 'Why not?'

'Well, when you did yesterday morning, Roffey overheard my telling you I couldn't talk any longer and would call you back.'

'So what?'

'I felt he thought we'd been behaving suspiciously.'

'It'd be far more unnatural if I did suddenly stop phoning you,' he said with a note of huffiness.

'Perhaps you're right.'

'And Sheila?'

'Yes.'

'When this is all over you will get another job, won't you?'

'You promised not to bring that up again.'

'I can't help it, I just hate your being there. Please say you'll hand in your notice and get right out of that whole starchy place. It's like a warrenful of bowler-hatted rabbits with public-school accents.'

Sheila gave him an indulgent smile. 'I can't leave yet, anyway, not until all this has been cleared up and for some time after that, so there's no point in talking about it.'

'I just want you to promise you'll leave as soon as you can.'

'Why should I be any hotter on promises than you?'

He glowered. 'That's not fair,' he said sulkily, 'particularly as none of this would have happened if you'd left before as I wanted you to.'

'One could also say,' Sheila said in a tone hoisted with warning signs, 'that none of this would have happened if you had ever learnt to control your temper.'

She moved out of his reach as she spoke just in case he took a swipe at her. It wouldn't have been the first time.

But he made no move and merely gave a slow nod. 'I am better than I used to be,' he said. 'You've helped me.'

'I'm not sure that I have,' Sheila replied, being in no

hurry to show that his contrition had melted her. 'Sometimes I think that I only stoke up your jealousy.'

'But I'm in love with you. Of course I'm jealous.'

'There's jealousy and jealousy. Both are bad, but the one which leads to violence is worse.'

He bit his lip. 'I'm sorry, Sheil, I really am. I promise I'll try much harder not to be jealous, or, at least, to conceal it, if you'll help me.'

She put out a hand and rested it on his foot. 'I'll help you,' she said, playing with one of his toes. 'It's been a rotten week for everyone. Let's hope the next one'll be better.'

'I can face it if I know you're with me, even though the bloody police are still nosing around me.'

'Just stick to what we've already told them and we've nothing to be frightened of.'

'Correct.' But his expression belied any confidence.

XVI

Philip Quant threw down the brief he had been trying to read and reached forward to turn on the television.

The brief was a complicated fraud relating to bills of exchange, some of which revolved and others of which were reissued. He had been trying without much success to understand the distinction. The trouble was that his instructing solicitor seemed equally hazy, which did not contribute to the clarity of his instructions. When the balloon had gone up, or the skies had fallen, the London branch of a faintly dubious Continental bank had let out a self-righteous squawk and the Fraud Squad had moved in. A year later proceedings had been launched against Quant's client and he was now awaiting trial at the Old Bailey. Since he was on bail the odds were that he would go on 'awaiting' for a good many months yet.

Nevertheless, distant though the date of trial might be, Quant had brought the brief back to read over the weekend for two reasons. First, because he never liked leaving briefs unread on his desk, however remote the trial and, secondly, because these particular papers looked as though they would serve to distract his mind from other matters which were currently preying on it. In this they failed, however, and so it was he turned to 'sports parade' on B.B.C. television in the hope that it would help to unwind him.

For half an hour he watched, but without concentration. He had the tight, desperate, reckless feeling that always came over him at moments of personal crisis. He recognised the weakness which induced it, but was generally powerless to break the spell. The greater the crisis, the stronger the compulsion to behave recklessly.

Sometimes he wondered what the end would be. Where would these self-destructive forces drive him? To suicide? He saw it as a possibility, though nothing greater at the moment. Then at other times when everything was going smoothly, the façade of the busy, respectable barrister was so firmly in place that even he could persuade himself it was reality right down through all the layers of his complex make-up.

He switched off the set and picked up the scattered papers of his brief from the floor and slipped back over them untied the length of pink tape. Then he wandered into the bathroom for no particular reason. But while there he decided to take a bath, as this sometimes had a relaxing effect on his nerves.

He made it as hot as he could bear and lay wallowing in the heavily steamed-up atmosphere. For a long time he made a dispassionate study of his body. It was a lean body from which bones protruded in answer to every movement. His stomach was flat and was no hairier now than it had been when he was eighteen. There was a small neat mat of hair on his chest. He really was disgustingly white and he wondered whether he should not buy a sun lamp. He pictured his body beautifully tanned and with a new suppleness.

After twenty minutes he began to feel sick and realised that the water had been too hot. He had better get out before he felt worse.

As he slowly dried himself, he decided what he would do. He would get dressed in something smart but casual and go out to a small club he knew. Even as he made the decision, he was aware that it had been predetermined since the onset of his present mood and he experienced a small tremor of excitement.

It was nearly six o'clock before he eventually left his flat. Spinning things out in anticipation was half the pleasure.

He caught a bus and alighted at Hyde Park Corner. It was a misty evening which contrived to enhance his feeling of anonymity and he walked slowly along Piccadilly glancing frequently about him.

'William's Place', which was the name of the club, had a discreet entrance off one of Mayfair's numerous alleyways. It was not far from Shepherd Market and it was into this street that he turned. He walked as far as Curzon Street and then along to the Curzon Cinema where he paused and affected interest in the frame of stills outside.

His darting glances had detected a number of men loitering in the area who would suddenly simulate intense interest in some shop window or other while their eyes, too, quickly appraised the immediate scene.

Quant wandered on, ignoring the inviting gaze of an unshaven young man of Mediterranean complexion, though he felt a small quiver of excitement as he passed close by him.

A little farther on, he stopped and studied the cards in an enclosed frame outside a newsagents. A 'dancing mistress' offered 'strictest tuition in the latest steps' and 'an attractive French girl' was available for 'private lessons'. In yet another a 'young male model' sought 'part-time employment'. Each advertisement was accompanied by a telephone number and Quant was filled with self-disgust when he realised he had memorised that of the young male model. He would drive it out of his mind immediately by mentally jumbling the figures around.

The barman at 'William's Place' stared at him suspiciously. He was new and Quant had not been to the club for about a couple of months.

'You're a member?'

'Yes. Name of Robinson.'

The barman glanced in a book he had out of sight behind the counter.

'*Mark* Robinson?'

'That's right.'

Reassured, his suspicion melted away at once. 'Fine. What do you want to drink, Mr Robinson?'

'I'll have a Campari soda.'

'Haven't seen you in here before, I don't think.'

'No, I don't come very often. You're new, too, aren't you?'

'Been here about six weeks. Orders are to be pretty careful and to question the credentials of anyone I don't know.' He glanced around the empty room, empty apart from a couple talking earnestly in one of the sub-fusc corners.

A good-looking youth (it could have been the 'young male model' of the advertising card) and an older man with a puffy, debauched face, thinning hair, and hands smothered with gold rings and bracelets facing each other with their noses almost touching. The youth was doing the talking while the man's only movement was an occasional twitch of his nose. The youth might have been breathing pure oxygen at him from the other's expression.

'Quiet this evening,' Quant said as he sipped his drink.

'It's early yet. They'll be in later.'

He had hardly spoken before a tall, willowy young man entered. He was handsome as a half-caste often can be and was wearing a frilly mauve silk shirt and a pair of purple velvet trousers which encased his buttocks as tightly as skin.

' 'Evening, Tony,' he said to the barman before giving

Quant an appraising glance. The barman retired into a room behind the bar to fetch a bottle.

Quant tore his own look away and concentrated on his glass.

'You waiting for anyone?' the young man asked. He had a soft drawl with a faint North American accent.

'No, but I have to go soon. I just dropped in for a quick one.'

The young man grinned impishly. 'I can give you a quick one if that's what you want.'

Philip Quant felt himself blushing furiously.

'Thanks, but I have to go now,' he said, with a note of panic in his voice. He downed his drink and turned rapidly away.

He could feel the half-caste smiling with impudent amusement at his discomfiture.

Out in the street, he scurried towards the seeming safety of Piccadilly. His leg felt flabby and he was bathed in perspiration.

How much longer, he wondered, could he play with fire without becoming burnt!

But had he not already been severely singed! Was that not the cause of his present predicament!

With a strange and unjustified feeling of release and relief, he walked to his very respectable club in Pall Mall and sat down to dinner in the company of lawyers and senior civil servants.

Dr Jekyll was once more firmly in control. Mr Hyde might never have been – until next time.

XVII

Adrian Slatter's taste in restaurants was considered by many who knew him to be as deplorable as his taste in girlfriends.

He had a penchant for picking noisy basement places with music where the food was pre-cooked, in so far as it was cooked at all, and the service ranged from casual to non-existent. All these imperfections being multiplied on a Saturday night when everything was stretched to the limit.

La Gonjonara, whose entrance was just off the King's Road, was one such establishment, and on this particular Saturday night even Adrian Slatter became restless as drinks failed to materialise, the wrong food was brought and the three singing guitarists who performed under the name of Los Moustachios (they did, in fact, all have heavy moustaches) remained permanently wedged beside his table which was closer than their skill warranted.

Around half past midnight, Los Moustachios took a rest and Slatter suggested to his companion that they should also leave. She was a girl named Paula whom he had met at a party about six weeks before. She had told him within a few minutes of their meeting how she had married the wrong man, how he had turned out to be a rotter and had gone off and left her flat.

He had evinced no particular interest in her background which, give or take a detail, was one common to most of his women friends. What had attracted him had been her figure and her line in daring conversation, with its promise (since fulfilled) of bedworthiness.

'Let's go,' he said, looking around unsuccessfully for their waiter.

'I like it here,' Paula said, 'and anyway it's early and to-morrow's Sunday.'

They were both slightly drunk to the extent of a slowing-down of the reactions.

'To-day's Sunday,' he said with a lop-sided smile.

'Why do you want to leave now, Adrian pet?'

'It's so hot! And the noise with those guitarists strumming and singing inside your eardrum!'

'I think they're very good. I like the big one in particular.'

'What do you like about him?'

She giggled. 'I just like him.'

'He's probably got a wife and six children,' he said, correctly divining the cause of her interest.

'I still like him.'

'Anyway, shall we go?'

'I'd like another brandy.'

'Do you really want one?'

'Yes.'

He looked round helplessly and by chance managed to catch the eye of the wine-waiter.

'Two more Cognacs, please.'

Having won her point, she was ready to propitiate him.

'I wish I'd met you sooner, pet, you could have handled my divorce.'

'I thought you weren't divorced.'

'Nobody seems to know,' she said vaguely. 'Godfrey just disappeared and the lawyer I spoke to said they'd have to find him before anything could be done.'

'But did you ever start divorce proceedings?'

'I signed some papers. Perhaps I am divorced!'

'Well, you'd know!'

'Can you find out for me pet?'

'You can't become divorced without knowing it,' Slatter said firmly, through the clearing mist of brandy fumes. He was not really drunk and he certainly didn't wish to get properly tight. It was a nuisance having to have a further brandy. However, he had proven ability to pull himself together at will provided he had not passed a mark which was still a long way ahead of him on this particular evening.

'My friend Julia did.'

'It must have been her fault. She can't have been paying attention.' They both broke out laughing.

'I do like your sense of humour, I always say that a man without humour is like a boiled egg without salt.' Her look challenged him to disagree as she added, 'Don't you think that's rather good?'

'Yes, very good,' he lied.

'I'd love to come and hear you in Court one day, Adrian.

I can just imagine you telling the old judge where he gets off.' She sipped daintily at her brandy which had come. 'You do wear a wig, don't you?'

'No. Only barristers do. I'm a solicitor.'

'Well, what's a lawyer then?'

'It covers both barristers and solicitors.'

'So you are a lawyer?'

'Yes.'

'But you told me you were defending this Manion man at the Old Bailey,' she said accusingly after a frowning pause. 'Manion man,' she repeated slowly as though savouring the alliteration.

'I'm his solicitor and I'm there in Court, but there's a barrister who actually conducts his case.'

'What's his name?' she asked suspiciously, before knocking back the remainder of her brandy.

'James Geddy.'

'What do you do, then? Just sit on your arse, if you'll pardon my Spanish?'

'Not quite ... I'll tell you on the way home. It's too difficult to explain in all this noise.'

'But I want to know.'

'I'll tell you on the way back.'

'I want to know now.'

'No.'

'I want another brandy.'

'No-o.'

'You're being horrid to me.'

It took a further twenty minutes to obtain the bill and persuade Paula to leave.

She lived in a block of flats in Kilburn, though she always referred to it as being West Hampstead, and when they arrived outside, Adrian Slatter leaned across her to open the passenger door.

She looked at him in surprise.

'That's not very polite of you, pet.'

'I'm not coming in this evening, Paula. I've got rather a headache. I'm going straight back to my own bed.'

151

Her look changed from surprise to outrage. 'Your own bed, indeed,' she said shrilly. 'That'll be the night, you little legal runt!'

Her heels tapped out their own angry endorsement of the comment as she crossed the pavement and disappeared inside the building.

Slatter sighed. He wished he could have spent the night with her, but first things first.

XVIII

P.C. Timms was twenty-one and had been in the force for a couple of years. He was a tall, well-built young man and regarded himself as fortunate in having a job he enjoyed so much. It seemed to him to provide endless variety and stimulation and his only reservation concerned the pay. He didn't feel that it took into sufficient account the risks and responsibility of a policeman's life. Several thousand other policemen shared his view.

In addition to enthusiasm, P.C. Timms had a healthy, robust attitude towards his duties and though he realised that an element of danger was implicit in the life, he had no anxieties or fears on this score.

He rather enjoyed being on night duty and keeping eyes and ears open for untoward sights and sounds.

It was shortly before three o'clock on Sunday morning when a light attracted his notice. If it had been an ordinary light on in a room, he would probably not have given it further attention. But it was the furtive beam of a torch somewhere at the back of a first-floor room of a mews flat near Baker Street.

P.C. Timms moved across to the opposite side of the road from where he could get a fuller view of the window through which he had seen the light. It was still on, but, like a nocturnal insect, had settled on something at the rear of the room.

He decided to move into the shadow of a doorway and watch. There was, of course, no earthly reason why a householder should not walk about his flat by torchlight at three in the morning, but it was unusual. If he was looking for something, why could he not turn on the light? Perhaps there was someone sleeping in the room whom the other person didn't wish to disturb.

As these thoughts passed through his head, the subdued light continued to be reflected from the back of the room.

He left his cover and walked back across the road to examine the entrance door. It was closed and there was no sign of it having been forced. It had a yale lock but no handle on the outside. P.C. Timms placed his gloved palm on the door and pushed, but it held fast.

He returned to the doorway on the opposite side and glanced back. The torchlight still showed, but now seemed to come from further to the right.

P.C. Timms considered the courses open to him. He could walk away and forget about it, and certainly nobody could hold anything against him if he did. He could ring the front-door bell and then explain to whoever answered what had prompted him to do so. Or he could continue keeping observation in the hope that somehow the problem would solve itself.

After several seconds deliberation, he decided that courses one and three were equally unsatisfactory and that he should adopt course two. It was clearly an occasion for positive rather than negative action. Thus decided, he walked straight over to the front-door and rang the bell. It sounded very loud in the absolute quietness of the night.

He stepped immediately back and stared up at the window. The torch beam had been extinguished and the window stared blindly back at him. He thought he detected some sort of movement in the room, but he couldn't be sure. Nevertheless, he was now certain that whoever was in the room had no right to be.

He suddenly remembered that these particular mews

flats had fire escapes at the rear which led into a narrow passage running parallel to the mews.

Glancing in each direction – it was an open-ended mews – he decided that it was equidistant whichever way he went and dashed off to his right.

He almost fell over rounding the corner at the end, but in a matter of half a minute, he was charging up the passage, sure that the intruder must make his exit here. But there was sign of neither life nor light. Everything remained still in the darkness.

Timms was certain that whoever it was could not already have made his escape.

For a second he paused, puzzled and frustrated, before plunging on to the far end of the passage. The road there was deserted and a few yards brought him back to the opposite end of the mews from which he had exited.

He was just in time to see a figure disappear round the corner at the far end. He pounded after it, but before he was half-way there he heard a car start up and accelerate away. And when he reached the street, everything was as silent as it had been a few seconds before.

He made an immediate report on his radio, though he knew nothing could now be done.

Later that night when he returned to the station for a refreshment break, the sergeant said to him, 'That place where you saw a light, it belongs to Manion; you know, the bloke that's on trial at the Old Bailey.'

XIX

'Those silk socks you bought the other week are in holes already, Father. How much did you pay for them?' Marion Roffey's expression as she stood in the doorway of the living-room of their bungalow reinforced the challenge of her tone.

'I can't remember, dear,' her father replied defensively

from behind the *Sunday Times*.

'Well, if you have any sense you'll take them back and complain.' She sniffed. 'But I don't suppose you will.' She was about to depart with the roundly condemned socks clutched in her hand when she turned back. 'I'm going out in a few minutes, Father, and may not be back till near bedtime.'

'Have a nice time, dear.'

'I'm going round to Gwen's. She's got Pamela and her mother and a dotty aunt coming to tea and supper and has asked me to help out.'

Chief Superintendent Roffey had no idea who Pamela was, let alone her mother or her dotty aunt. He didn't doubt that he had been told at one time or another, but this, together with much of what his daughter told him, would have passed in one ear and out of the other.

Since becoming a widower six years before, his daughter Marion had kept house for him, though that was but a small part of her busy life.

She was a Higher Executive Officer in the Civil Service, working in one of the more prosaic departments of government and, in addition to that and looking after her father, she was a member of the local madrigal society and currently taking evening classes in pottery and Italian. Last year it had been free art and Spanish and the year before drama and French. She also participated in a number of extramural activities run by the Civil Service.

Although she was only just thirty, she appeared older and could best be summed up as the reverse of frivolous. She was constantly expressing disapproval of her father's sartorial extravagances, though without effect. She was probably the only person who had never felt remotely overawed by him. He realised this and had long since capitulated to the inevitable, though not to the extent of an open admission.

He had spent most of Saturday in his office reading through all the statements which had been taken. He had done this not once, nor even twice, but three times, knowing that it is often by reading, re-reading and cross-checking statements that new lines of enquiry emerge. Not that anything so profitable had happened on this occasion.

He had spent the latter part of the day following up one or two hunches about the case, but, once again, without any positive result. This, however, didn't cause him to discard his theories.

Philip Quant was still his quarry in the sense that greater suspicion seemed to attach to him than to anyone else. He had lied and his lies must be nailed. And when they were nailed, the odds were that the case would be solved.

As to that girl typist, she, too, had been at pains to conceal the truth from him so far as it touched her boy-friend. Roffey didn't share Detective Sergeant Chisett's suspicion of Alan Dixon. Even if he did have a temper and was of a jealous nature, he couldn't see him committing this particular murder. If he had suddenly come on Sheila and young Appleman in bed together, he might have killed him, but not as he sat alone in a room in Chambers. Roffey paused as he reflected that there was no evidence Appleman was alone at the time the murderer came upon him. Though equally there was no evidence that he was not.

And then there was George Uppard who would probably scruple less at murder than any of the others. He had the opportunity, but no known motive. And whoever murdered Robin Appleman had most surely had a motive with a capital M.

But even if he was wrong in his pet hunch, he was still absolutely certain that the murderer came from among those he had already interviewed. And this meant reinterviews and yet further interviews with that small circle until suddenly something he was told stood out like a throbbing red beacon.

Maybe he would get a lucky break, though generally you had to work hard for your breaks and for the so-called luck that often accompanied them.

He heard the front door close and saw Marion walk down the short path to the street. She moved briskly and purposefully. Not for the first time, he reflected that she would have made a good woman police officer. He had once told her so, to be met my mirthless scorn.

He laid down the newspaper and reached for his brief-case. He would read through all the statements again.

To-morrow was Monday and there was no time to lose. He must not allow the momentum of his enquiries to slacken. If he had not made an arrest by the end of the coming week, the outlook would be grim indeed.

As he emerged from the Bank Underground Station shortly before nine o'clock the next morning, he paused, as he always did, and glanced about him with the feeling of exhilaration and pride that this was the heart of the City of London for whose protection and well-being he carried part responsibility. He looked from the Mansion House to the Royal Exchange and on to the Bank of England as though to satisfy himself that none of them had been nicked over the weekend before setting off at a brisk walk to his office in Old Jewry. To his pleasure he was recognised and greeted twice on his way. Once by a bank manager of the city branch of one of the big five and the other time by a member of Lloyds. Both of them men of substance in the City's commercial life.

On arrival at headquarters his progress was marked by the usual punctuation of 'good morning, sirs' which he acknowledged as usual with a mild flip of his umbrella.

In his other hand he was carrying his brief-case – not an official one but an elegantly thin executive's case with two locks which snapped more crisply than a breakfast cereal.

He had not long been in his room when there was a knock on the door and a young P.C. in uniform entered.

'I was asked to bring this up to you straight away, sir,' he said, handing Roffey a letter. 'Sergeant Preston thought it might be to do with your murder case.'

Roffey took the letter with a nod of thanks and the P.C. departed after a slight pause to see whether his curiosity as to its contents was going to be satisfied.

Something caused Roffey to study the outside carefully

before attempting to open it.

He noticed that the postmark was W.1 and that it had been posted on Sunday. In the top left-hand corner it was marked 'personal and private'. His name and the address were also printed in capitals and it struck him immediately that they were correct in every faultless detail, even to his own mouthful of a rank being correctly spelt out. Everything had been printed with a ballpoint pen and he continued to gaze at the envelope with interest before slitting it carefully open with a small silver penknife which he always carried.

Then holding it upside down he shook out the contents consisting apparently of a snapshot which landed face down on his desk.

He left it there for a moment while he peered into the envelope to make sure it contained nothing further. It did not.

Picking the snapshot up cautiously by its edges he turned it over. At the same moment Detective Sergeant Chisett came into the room. His chief's expression stilled the pleasantry which was on his lips.

Roffey was staring at the snapshot with wide-eyed astonishment. Indeed, Chisett could not ever recall seeing such an expression of gaping surprise on the face of his Detective Chief Superintendent.

'What've you got there, sir?' he asked in a tone of polite interest after Roffey had failed to recognise his presence.

Roffey laid the snapshot down carefully on his desk.

'What do you make of this, then?' he said, leaning back and shooting Chisett the sort of beady look an examiner might bestow on a victim at a practical test.

Sergeant Chisett moved closer, stared down at the photograph and let out a low whistle of astonishment.

'It's Slatter, sir.'

'Certainly it's Slatter.'

'But who's the girl?'

'I've no idea. That's something we shall find out. This morning. By asking him.'

Chisett's glance went to the envelope. 'But who on earth can have sent you this photograph of Slatter and a very dead-looking girl?'

'I'm more interested in the conjunction of Slatter with a dead girl,' Roffey said in his more pompous voice.

'He's bending right over her body,' Chisett remarked.

'Precisely.'

XX

It was some time before Sergeant Chisett recalled that he had had a reason for coming to Roffey's room. When he remembered, he said:

'I've got something to show you, too, sir.'

He handed Roffey the letter which Mrs Appleman had sent her son and which had been found and opened by David and Holly on their furtive visit to his flat.

The top of the envelope had been slit and Roffey extracted the letter and read it. When he finished he glanced up at Chisett.

'I found it at the deceased's place,' Chisett explained. 'I went along there on Saturday evening to see the landlord and he handed it to me.'

'Opened?'

'No, I opened it. I phoned Appleman's home and found out that it must be the letter his mother had sent him and I asked her if I could open it after she'd told me it referred to a row he'd had with someone in Chambers which he had written home about. It obviously ties in with the diary entry, sir.'

'With Quant,' Roffey said in a thoughtful tone, adding after a pause, 'He's certainly not out of the wood as far as I'm concerned. However, let's get along to the Bailey and catch Slatter before he goes into Court.'

Roffey decided that, at that hour of a Monday morning,

they would get there as quickly on foot as in a car and gave instructions that the car should come along at its own crawling pace and wait for them to complete their business at the Court.

Meanwhile, he and Chisett set off at a brisk pace on the short walk along Poultry, Cheapside and Newgate Street.

Roffey's step was purposeful and his air proprietorial and it seemed natural that others should make way for him. Sergeant Chisett, however, found himself frequently sidestepping, dropping back and generally moving like a poorly articulated crab to Roffey's king swordfish.

'Good morning, gentlemen,' a voice called out as they were going up the entrance steps of the Court building.

They turned to find George Uppard just behind them.

'Good morning,' Roffey said briskly. 'Is Mr Slatter here yet?'

Uppard glanced at him with what could have been an expression of secret amusement and shook his head. ''Fraid not. He's not coming to the Bailey to-day. No real need for him to attend as there's only the summing-up, but he's not feeling too well anyway. That's why I've come along.' He looked from one to the other with a cocked eyebrow. 'Anything I can do to assist you, gentlemen?'

'I wanted to have a word with Mr Slatter.'

'You'll find him in the office. Though on second thoughts you'd better ring first as he may have gone off home.'

'What's wrong with him?' Chisett enquired.

'Couldn't really find out,' Uppard said airily. 'He looked fairly rotten; though, between ourselves, he quite often does on a Monday morning.' This remark was accompanied by a sly wink. 'That's the trouble with these young bachelors! Too much g and t over the weekend.'

'G and t?'

'Gin and tits!' Uppard laughed delightedly at his witticism. 'Anyway, like me to phone the office and find out if he's still there?'

'Don't bother. We'll take a chance,' Roffey said. 'If he's not in the office, we'll go on to his home.'

'Something important cropped up, has it?' Uppard asked with undisguised interest.

'Just something I want to check with Mr Slatter personally.'

Uppard looked amused. 'Well, I mustn't hold you up. Also, I'd better go and wait upon our illustrious client on the last day of the trial.'

'What's going to happen to him?' Chisett asked.

'It's what's going to happen to his poor solicitors if he doesn't get off,' Uppard said breezily. 'He'll want our skins for lampshades!'

'He seems more pleased with himself than usual,' Chisett remarked after Uppard had left them.

'Possibly,' Roffey replied without interest. 'He's never exactly retiring.'

Their car arrived a few minutes later and they drove westwards to the Strand.

A girl in a mini-skirt with legs like piano stools received them at Finster, Slatter & Co.

'Do you have an appointment?' she asked when Roffey said they wished to see Mr Slatter.

'No, but say it's Detective Chief Superintendent Roffey and Detective Sergeant Chisett.'

'How do you spell Roff-whatever you said?'

'R-O-F-F-E-Y,' Roffey replied with asperity.

'And the other gentleman?'

'Just tell him Chief Superintendent Roffey wants to see him urgently.' Roffey's tone was impatient.

'I'm only doing what I'm told.'

'I'm sure you are! Now, be a good girl and go and tell Mr Slatter I'm here.'

She threw them a doubtful glance and disappeared to return a minute later and announced, 'Mr Slatter will see you now.' Her tone seemed to convey that she had worked a small miracle for which they should all give thanks.

Adrian Slatter rose as they were shown into his office and motioned them to a couple of chairs. Uppard had not over-stated the case when he had said that his principal looked rotten. There were dark rings round his eyes, his skin had a yellowish tinge and he had had an obviously rough shave.

'I gather you're not feeling very well this morning,' Roffey said, looking at Slatter across the small, cheerless room as though in some way challenging him either to leap up and deny it or to slither in a coma to the floor.

'I've got a migraine,' Slatter said in a deadened tone. 'But what is it you want to see me about?'

For a second or two, Roffey just stared at him in silence. 'This!' he said, suddenly pulling the snapshot from his pocket and thrusting it under Slatter's gaze.

Slatter blinked, swallowed painfully and then slowly closed his eyes while his complexion took on an even yellower tint.

As he observed him, it occurred to Chisett that they were watching a man who was drawing his last few breaths and who was about to drift across the threshold between life and death.

'Mr Slatter, are you all right?' Roffey said sharply.

He was on the point of getting out of his chair when Slatter very slowly opened his eyes again.

'Where did this come from?' he asked dully.

'It came into my possession.'

'You won't tell me how?'

'I see no reason to disclose that at this stage.'

Slatter nodded wearily. 'I see.'

He picked the photograph up and examined the reverse side. 'From the fact that you let me touch it, I gather it has no fingerprints?' He gave them a small sour smile.

'Perhaps you'd care to explain it,' Roffey said with a trace of impatience.

'Oh, that's not very difficult. It was taken some years ago when I was staying in Hamburg. I went to a party. A very strange party, full of very kinky people and we played a form of charades and a creepy little man with a small black beard took flashlight photographs of the various turns. He later sent me a couple of copies. This must be one of them.'

'What were you supposed to be portraying?' Roffey asked suspiciously.

Slatter looked embarrassed. 'May I assume that this is all in confidence, Mr Roffey?'

'Provided it turns out to have no bearing on my enquiry, it won't go any farther.'

'That's fair! We were supposed to be enacting a sex murder.' He looked from Roffey to Chisett and appeared wryly amused by their expressions of surprise.

'Are you saying that this girl in the photo wasn't really dead?'

'She got up afterwards, so I don't think she can have been.'

Roffey frowned at the intrusion of such facetiousness.

'Who was she?' he asked sharply.

'I've no idea. I'd never seen her before and I've never seen her since.'

'Where was this party held?'

'I'm afraid I can't help you with that, either. I've long since forgotten the address.'

'How did you come to attend it?'

'I'd met a German girl at a night-club the previous evening and she suggested I should go along.'

'What was her name?'

Slatter shook his head. 'If I ever knew, I certainly don't any longer. She was just a casual pick-up.'

'And this night-club where you met her?'

'Somewhere off the Reeperbahn. You've heard of the Reeperbahn? It's where all the sleazy dives are. Every perversion catered for in half a mile.'

'And what's yours, Mr Slatter?' Roffey asked, with what was almost a snarl.

'I'm straight.'

Roffey managed to bite back the further comment he felt stung to make. 'When was this Hamburg incident?'

'Four years ago this last autumn.'

'What were you doing there?'

'I was there on business. I can give you the particulars if

you want.'

'Later, maybe.' He had no doubt that Slatter had made such a visit at the time he said. To accept his offer to authenticate his trip would merely enhance his morale further. 'You said just now that the man who took this photograph of you and this half-naked girl sent you a couple of copies and that this must be one of them?' Slatter nodded. 'Where did you keep these copies?'

'In a drawer at home. I don't suppose you'd know this, but my flat was burgled last winter. Nothing much was taken – some money, a camera, a watch – but whoever it was went through every drawer in the place and I afterwards found these photos were missing. For obvious reasons, I didn't list them among the property which was stolen. Apart from anything else, they had no intrinsic value.'

A silence fell which was broken when Roffey got up abruptly. 'That seems to be all for the moment, Mr Slatter.'

'Are you prepared to tell me *now* how this print came into your possession?'

Roffey paused. 'I received it anonymously through the post.'

'I guessed as much,' Slatter remarked in a grim tone.

'How?'

'If you'd got it from a known person, I presume you wouldn't have indulged in such an obvious fishing expedition?'

'Perhaps *you* can suggest who may have sent it to me?'

'I wish I could. The obvious person is my unknown burglar, but I'm afraid that's not a very helpful suggestion.'

'No, I'm afraid it's not.'

Sergeant Chisett could not help reflecting as they descended the dingy, narrow staircase to the street that the interview which for them had begun as a rout of their quarry had ended as a rearguard action.

XXI

Donald was again trying to make three phone calls at once. Sheila who was holding on for one of them covered the mouthpiece and said:

'I've got Hodges and Bendon on the line, who is it you want to speak to?'

'Mr Plater, the clerk who looks after their criminal work.'

A second later, Sheila handed him the telephone.

'Mr. Plater? Bob, this is Donald, Mr Quant's clerk. I'm afraid we're in a bit of difficulty about your case at Middlesex Sessions to-day. I've just had a call from Mr Quant saying that he's sick and won't be able to cope. I can do one of two things, Bob. Phone the Court and explain and send someone along to ask for an adjournment or, if you'd prefer it, get Mr Ilford to take over the brief. It's only a plea in mitigation and there's not much reading in it, so Mr Ilford could probably do it as well as Mr Quant if you're agreeable. Terribly sorry, Bob, but there we are ... Mr Ilford? Oh, he's very good, I'm sure you'd have no cause to grumble. He's been in Chambers about five years ... junior to Mr Quant, but doing extremely well. Just happens that a case of his to-day has fallen through so he's free ... O.K., Bob, I'll warn him now and get him along to Court right away. It's marked not before twelve o'clock, so that'll give him and you and the lay client time to have a con. My apologies again, Bob, and thanks for understanding my difficulty. ... What's that? No, you're right, it certainly hasn't added to the joy of my life, but we just have to keep on soldiering with fingers crossed ... Anyway, thanks for your sympathy ... Bye, Bob.'

Donald replaced the receiver and let out a sigh of relief.

'I'll nip along and tell Mr Ilford and get the brief from

Mr Quant's table. See if you can get me the solicitors in that appeal case of Mr Ainsworth's. The Court now want to change the date and bring it forward a week. Also try and get me the Clerk of Assize office at Kingston, I want them to put that case of Mr Geddy's in the list to-morrow, if possible . . .'

*　　*　　*

Philip Quant knew that Anthea Rayner avoided, as far as possible, working on Monday mornings. She had private means and was not dependent on her income at the Bar, and this enabled her to be rather more selective in her work than others. For her, the Bar was an extremely agreeable life, but she was not fired by any burning ambition and ordered her work so that it did not consume all her time and energies. If she declined to take a brief, there was always someone in Chambers who was pleased to accept it after Donald had fixed things with the solicitors. The net result was that her competence ensured a regular flow of work and her independent means protected her against becoming a slave to too much.

Thus it was in the reasonably certain knowledge of finding her at home that Quant phoned her flat shortly after informing Donald of his intended defection from Middlesex Sessions.

'Anthea, this is Philip. I'd very much like to come round and see you. I'd sooner not say anything more on the phone, but may I come straight away?'

If Anthea Rayner was surprised, she didn't reveal it on the telephone. 'Yes, certainly Philip. I'll be at home all morning.'

'I'll get a taxi and come at once.'

Twenty minutes later, he was sitting in her expensively-furnished but comfortable living-room. She had made some coffee and handed him a cup. She could see that he was tense and on edge and decided that it was up to her to make the emergence of the reason for his visit as easy as possible. As she watched him fidgeting with his cup and constantly running his tongue round the inside of his mouth, she saw herself as a sort of spiritual midwife.

'I take it,' she said in a calming voice, 'that you've got some sort of problem you want to talk about?'

'Yes, but now I'm here, I don't know where to begin. Perhaps I shouldn't have come after all. Why should I burden you with my ghastly troubles?'

'You'll probably feel better if you do unburden yourself and the odds are they're not as ghastly as you imagine.'

'Oh, don't have any illusions on that score,' he said bitterly. 'I'm in terrible trouble and you're the only person I feel I can talk to. You're calm and sensible and will know what I should do.'

'Is it something to do with Robin Appleman's murder?' she enquired.

'Yes. I think the police may suspect me.' He looked at her anxiously, but she said nothing and her expression remained one of quiet interest. 'You see, I had a beastly row with Appleman shortly before his death and the police have found out because he wrote about it in his diary. At least he referred to it without saying what it was about.'

'But naturally the police wanted to know what it was about?'

'Yes.'

'And you told them?'

'I gave them a reason.'

'But not the true one, is that it?'

He nodded. 'I told them it was because he had been importuning me to help him get a tenancy in Chambers.'

Anthea frowned. 'He hadn't really been doing that, had he?'

'No.'

'Then what *was* the row about?'

Quant buried his face in his hands and his whole body shook while terrible strangulated sounds came from his throat.

Anthea watched him for several seconds, then got up and came across to where he was sitting and put a hand on his shoulder.

'Try and pull yourself together, Philip, and then you'd better tell me the worst.'

XXII

For Detective Chief Superintendent Roffey, Monday morning passed with painful slowness after its initial impetus of promise. The two people he wanted to see were involved in the Manion trial and were, so to speak, beyond his reach until the lunch adjournment.

His immediate reaction on leaving Slatter's office had been that the snapshot was just a large red-herring which some mischief-maker had thrown across their trail. It had been remarkable the way Slatter had rallied after the first knock-out shock of seeing the photo. His explanation, if reflecting no credit on himself, was plausible and certainly didn't disclose any criminal conduct on his part.

Yes, plausible was the word. Whatever could be checked of what he had told them would doubtless prove to be true. What couldn't be checked might be true or might not ... If untrue, the blend with truth was so skilful and cunning as to defy detection.

These had been the lines on which his thoughts had run as he and Chisett drove away from the office of Finster, Slatter & Co. And then suddenly two apparently random thoughts entered his mind at the same moment and he sat bolt upright in the car and said, to Chisett's astonishment, 'Never ignore the obvious, because that's what we've been guilty of.'

At one o'clock, Mr Justice Tyler adjourned the Court after informing the jury that he had only a sentence to add to his summing-up before sending them out to consider their verdict. He explained that, by doing this, they could have their lunch under normal conditions and await their confinement in the jury room until after their stomachs had been appeased.

Roffey stepped forward as James Geddy left the Courtroom.

'I'm sorry to waylay you yet again, Mr Geddy, but there are just two further matters I want to ask you about.'

'Go ahead,' Geddy replied, with a touch of weariness.

'How would you describe Mr Appleman's approach to his work?'

It was clear from James Geddy's expression that it was the last sort of question he had been expecting.

'He was extremely conscientious and hard-working.'

'Did he express any views about this particular case?'

'You mean Manion?' Roffey nodded. 'Not that I recall. He was interested in it as he was in all my cases. He made a very good note for me before the trial started and he noted the evidence of all the witnesses when it was under way.' He gave Roffey a questioning look.

'What I'm really wondering,' Roffey said slowly, 'is whether he'd have been likely to have read those further papers which were delivered at your Chambers on the evening he met his death.'

'I should think it's more than likely he did. It would certainly have been in the nature of things for him to have done so. Not,' Geddy added, 'that there was anything in them which turned out to be of any help to the defence.'

'Of course, he volunteered to stay on and wait for their arrival, didn't he?'

'Yes, though I doubt whether that can be strictly attributed to his interest in the case.'

'You mean it was because he wanted to have an excuse to stay late in Chambers while Sheila was there.'

'Something like that,' Geddy said dryly.

Roffey was thoughtful for a time. 'I'd very much like to have a word with Manion himself during the adjournment, would you have any objection?'

'I wouldn't have any, but it's not really a matter for me. It's primarily a question for Manion himself. If he doesn't want to see you, that's that. You'd better speak to Mr Uppard, who is my instructing solicitor's managing clerk.'

'Yes, I know him, but I'd prefer not to speak to him.'

'It's like that, is it?'

'I'm not quite sure how it is. I'm playing a hunch and I'd sooner not let George Uppard in on the act.'

'Hmm! Well, it's not for me to probe your secrets, but why don't you wait for the trial to end? I doubt whether the jury'll be out very long and the odds are the whole thing will be over by three o'clock then presumably it's a matter entirely between you and Manion, or between you and the prison authorities and Manion.'

Roffey gave a wintry smile.

'Which do you think it'll be, Mr Geddy?'

'Between ourselves, Mr Roffey, I think he'll go down and, even more between ourselves, I hope he does!'

*   *   *

As events turned out, James Geddy's private hope was fulfilled just five minutes after the predicted hour.

The jury took forty-five minutes to reach their verdict, Geddy made a short but admirable plea in mitigation from which no one in court could have divined his personal feelings towards his client and the judge with the minimum of judicial sententiousness sentenced him to eighteen months' imprisonment. It was generally felt to be about the right sentence, and Detective Chief Superintendent Peters, the officer in charge of the case, was relieved to see even a small part of his original case successfully salvaged.

Manion himself accepted the verdict and sentence without any outward sign of emotion apart from a sudden compression of his lips and a fleeting expression of cold anger.

Roffey, who was sitting in one of the rows behind counsel observed George Uppard enter the dock after his client had been taken to the cells and follow him down the narrow staircase.

Mr Justice Tyler had begun trying another case while Manion's jury were out and he now continued with it.

Roffey, who knew that Uppard would have to emerge by way of the same staircase which led into the rear of the dock, sat back and waited.

Ten minutes later Uppard appeared, was ushered out of the custodial precincts and tiptoed from the Court without a glance in Roffey's direction. Roffey rose from his seat and made his own tip-toeing way to the dock where the Chief Prison Officer, to whom he had spoken during the lunch adjournment, opened the small door to admit him. A second later he was in the corridor of cells which ran beneath the Court.

The Chief Prison Officer who had accompanied him said, 'If he doesn't want to see you, I'm afraid there's nothing I can do about it.'

'I realise that. I've written him a note. Will you give it to him?'

Roffey handed the half sheet of Court stationery on which he had written:

'I am in charge of the enquiry into Appleman's death (Mr Geddy's barrister pupil) and should very much like to have a word with you. I think you may be able to help me.

R. Roffey, Detective Chief Superintendent.'

If Roffey was not surprised by the reply he received, the Prison Officer clearly was.

'Yes, he'll talk to you,' he said in a tone which indicated that this was not the message he had expected to bring back.

Manion was still holding the note between his fingers when Roffey was admitted to his cell.

'I've seen you in Court a few times,' he said in a matter-of-fact tone. 'In what way do you think I can help you?'

'I'll come to that in a minute. In principle are you willing to help?'

'That depends, doesn't it? If you think I'm going to hold my hand up and say I murdered the bloke, then obviously you can start thinking again.'

171

'Whoever did murder him, it couldn't have been you.'

'I'm glad to hear it, because I was wondering. I thought perhaps you were going to suggest I sneaked out of Brixton Prison for a couple of hours, committed a murder and sneaked back in again without anyone being the wiser. It wouldn't be beyond some of your colleagues to try that on,' he added with a sudden note of anger.

Roffey reached into his pocket and produced the photograph of Adrian Slatter and the unknown girl. Holding it out to Manion, he said, 'Ever seen that before?'

'I might have.'

'It was sent to me through the post, anonymously.'

Manion shrugged as though this information was of no particular interest to him.

'Who's the girl in the photo?'

For several seconds Manion flicked at the note Roffey had sent him and which he was still holding in one hand. The cell seemed to be filled with the sharp, vicious sound of his nail striking the paper.

'Look, Mr Roffey,' he said, suddenly letting go of the piece of paper and watching it flutter to the floor. 'You probably know enough about me to realise that I'm not someone who helps your lot unless it suits my book. I don't seek your help and I don't offer the police mine ... *unless*.'

'Unless what?'

'Just unless.'

'I don't follow you.'

Manion sat suddenly forward and fixed Roffey with a hard stare. 'O.K., let's not waste any more time. Perhaps I can help you solve your case, but how much of what I tell you I'm later prepared to put in writing depends ... well, just depends. Let's have it clear that I'm not talking because I want to assist the police. I'm talking because someone deserves what's coming to him.'

'You mean the person who murdered Appleman?'

Manion made a scornful sound. 'That's for you to bloody find out. I'm not a detective. *I* don't know who murdered him.'

'Then what *do* you know?'

Manion glanced quickly round the cell. 'This cell's not bugged, is it?'

'Definitely not.'

'Good. Then what passes here is just between you and me. And you can put your bloody notebook away, too!'

For the next quarter of an hour, Manion talked while Roffey listened intently. Only the shine in his eyes gave away his sense of mounting excitement.

Maybe Manion genuinely didn't know who had killed Robin Appleman, but Roffey grew more certain of the murderer's identity as various parts of the puzzle began to click comfortably into place.

XXIII

Holly looked round the door of Philip Quant's room where David was sitting alone at the desk noting up a brief.

'Philip not about?' she asked as he looked up.

'He hasn't been all day. He's sick.' Lowering his voice he said, 'Come in and close the door.' She did so and he went on, 'There's something funny going on. Donald looks harassed and keeps on popping into Martin's room. When I asked him what was wrong with Philip and when would he be back, he became all uncommunicative as though I was trying to wrest an official secret from him.'

'What do you imagine has happened to Philip?'

'It can only be something to do with the police enquiry.'

'But what?'

'What do you think?' David asked bleakly.

'Surely they can't suspect him of murdering Robin.'

'Why not? The police have probably got that letter by now. But, in any event, they'll have learnt of its contents from his parents. We know they've been in touch with them.'

'But that's not enough to justify a charge of murder.'

'True, but then we don't know what else they've found out. When they add all their bits and pieces together, they may decide that they do have enough.'

'It's possible he's got flu,' Holly said unconvincingly.

'Donald would have told me if that were so. No need for him to act mysteriously just because someone in Chambers has flu.'

'You could be imagining that he's acting mysteriously.'

'I could be, but I'm not.'

'After all,' Holly went on, 'it's very easy to lose one's sense of perspective after all Chambers has been through in the last week.'

'How's yours then?'

'My sense of perspective? I think it's O.K. at the moment.'

'So's mine,' David said firmly.

'Have you seen Anthea to-day?'

Holly shook her head. 'No. As you know, she often doesn't appear on Mondays. I went and sat behind Martin in the Court of Appeal, his junior had to dash off to the Bailey half-way through the appeal, but there was nothing for him to do anyway, still less for me, except make a note which no one was going to want.'

'Interesting case?'

'It was only an appeal against sentence. The chap had got three years for burglary and Martin got them to reduce it to eighteen months.'

'Nice for the chap, anyway!'

'He wasn't there to hear it.'

'They'll probably tell him.' They grinned at each other. 'The Governor'll have him up one morning and say, "Glad to tell you, Smith, we've just got the form through saying the Court of Appeal has halved your sentence. Sorry there's been a bit of a hold-up with it but luckily we're only a few weeks past your new release date." '

Holly was still giggling when the door opened and Donald came in. 'Is that the Poynter brief you're reading, sir?'

he asked, with a worried expression.

'No, Poynter's that fat wad of paper at the far end of the window seat.'

Donald hurried over and picked up the brief. He was about to leave the room when he turned round and said, 'By the way, Mr March, I think Mr Ainsworth wants to have a word with you.'

'Now?'

'Yes.'

David gave Holly a questioning look as he got up and followed Donald out of the room.

Martin Ainsworth's room was not particularly large, but it had the nicest view of any in Chambers, facing on to an expanse of one of the Temple's well-manicured lawns.

'Have a chair, David,' he said, his tone that of someone who feels himself hemmed in by problems. His gaze rested for a moment almost longingly on the side-table where about two dozen briefs of assorted sizes were piled, then his eyes came back to where David was sitting. 'I'm afraid our troubles are not yet over, David. Indeed they give the impression of multiplying.' He paused and stared at his fingertips. Then he said abruptly, 'If you have no objection, and I don't suppose you will, I think it would be a good idea if you transferred yourself as a pupil to James Geddy. James, I may add, will be delighted to take you over.' He paused and seemed to have difficulty in finding the right words. 'You see, I'm afraid Philip won't be back for a little while. He's not been well recently and now things seem to have got on top of him and he's going right away for a time.'

'I'm sorry he's not well,' David said, aware of the inadequacy of his own words, but Martin's own obvious embarrassment was catching.

'We can only hope that a complete change will do the trick.'

'Where's he going?'

'Switzerland, I understand. He's off to-morrow.'

'Switzerland! To-morrow!'

Martin nodded. 'Now you can understand why I began by saying that our troubles were not yet over?'

'But this is all so sudden,' David said boldly. 'It's almost as if he's running away from something.'

Martin Ainsworth looked at him sharply. 'What exactly do you mean, David?'

'Going abroad at a few hours' notice and at a time like this . . .' David's voice faltered as the extent of his boldness smacked him in the face.

'You're thinking that Robin Appleman's death and Philip's departure are connected in some way?'

'I'm not quite sure what I'm thinking!' By now he was thoroughly embarrassed.

'I'm afraid they are connected,' Martin said gravely.

David felt himself break out into a clammy sweat. He looked down at his body as though it was divorced from his conscious self. Somewhere at the back of his mind he reflected this must be how you would feel if a doctor suddenly told you that you had only a few months to live.

He was still in a state of shock when the door burst open and Donald came in, his hair falling across his forehead and his face suffused with emotion.

'I've just heard, sir, that the police have taken someone in and he's being questioned at the station now. It's Mr Slatter, sir.'

XXIV

Twenty-four hours later, Roffey paid a visit to 4 Mulberry Court.

He strode in hatted and umbrella-ed and Donald popped out of the clerks' room to greet him. Roffey gave him a brief nod as though to emphasise that his business was with the Head of Chambers and not with clerks. Stephen, who had come to the door of their room, didn't even receive a nod.

'I'll tell Mr Ainsworth you're here,' Donald said eagerly.

He hurried away while Roffey affected a polite interest in the shelves of law books which lined one wall of the entrance lobby, aware that several people were hovering in the vicinity in the hope of gleaning the inside story of what had led to Slatter being charged with Robin's murder, a circumstance which was briefly reported in the stop-press of the evening papers.

A minute later, Donald returned and escorted him to Martin's room, leaving an unsatisfied posse to continue with their private speculations.

'Come in and sit down, Mr Roffey,' Martin said affably, 'I thought you wouldn't mind Mr Geddy hearing what you have to say.'

'Very appropriate that he should be here in the circumstances,' Roffey replied, laying his hat and umbrella on one of the chairs and then sitting down. 'I've just seen the Under-Treasurer of the Inn and told him, also as a matter of courtesy, what I would propose to impart to you two gentlemen.'

'I gather that Slatter has now been charged?' Martin said.

'That's correct Mr Ainsworth and' – here he permitted himself an indulgent smile – 'I blame myself entirely for not having got on to him sooner. The trouble was, to use a colloquialism, I took my eye off the ball. I allowed myself to be distracted by a red-herring or two, though I don't believe that anyone else would have failed to have had their attention deflected from what stood out as the most significant feature of the case.' He glanced from one to the other of his audience, enjoying their puzzled expressions. I am referring, of course, to the absence of any fingerprints on the papers which Slatter's clerk brought here that night and handed to Mr Appleman. In the first place one might have expected to have found Slatter's or Uppard's and in the second Appleman's because, as Mr Geddy has since confirmed, he would certainly have read this new material that was supposed to be so important to Manion's defence. But there wasn't the vestige of a fingerprint on any of the several pieces of paper.'

'What's more they weren't remotely helpful to my case,' James Geddy put in.

Roffey smiled knowingly. 'That, too, is now susceptible of explanation,' he said. 'But first about the fingerprints. Why weren't there any?'

'Because someone had wiped them off,' Martin answered.

'Exactly,' Roffey said as though lauding a promising pupil in the classroom. 'And why should anyone have done that?'

'Because he didn't wish it known that the papers had been read?' This time it was James Geddy who replied.

'And why not?'

'You tell us,' Martin said, dryly.

'Because they had contained a vital clue.'

'What sort of a clue?' Geddy asked with a frown.

Roffey's expression was that of a conjuror about to pull off his most spectacular trick.

'A snapshot,' he said. 'A snapshot showing Slatter bending over the body of a dead, half-dressed girl. A snapshot taken by your recent client, Mr Geddy, when he and Slatter were on a business trip to Zurich a couple of years ago. It seems that Slatter picked this girl up in a bar one evening – she was a Swede, incidentally – went back to her room for the purpose of intercourse and then managed to kill her in the course of what one might call a bit of sexual rough and tumble. In a panic he hurried back to the hotel where he and Manion were staying, told Manion what had happened and enlisted his assistance in removing any tell-tale traces connecting him with the affair. Back at the scene, Manion took this photograph of him with the body. I don't mean that Slatter posed for it; indeed, I gather he was more than upset when he realised it had been taken, not that that would bother Manion. At all events they left Switzerland the next day and the girl's death has remained a mystery to the Swiss police ever since. She was known to be promiscuous and it was assumed that a pick-up had killed her, but there were absolutely no clues to his identity.'

'How did she die?' Martin asked.

'Vagal inhibition as a result of pressure on the neck.'

'So he probably didn't mean to kill her?'

'Manslaughter at the most by our law,' Roffey said, self-importantly.

'I would think so,' Martin agreed with a faint smile.

'Anyway,' Roffey went on, 'Manion kept the negative and some prints of this highly significant photograph against the day when they might prove useful to him – and that day came with his recent trial. It seems that he realised he was likely to be convicted of the last Count in the indictment unless he could get Slatter to concoct and ante-date a copy letter purporting to be to the victim of the attempted deception which would supposedly put him in the clear as far as any criminal intent was concerned. But Slatter was reluctant to be drawn into what in effect would be a criminal offence on his part. Forgery, in fact, with the further possibility of perjury to follow. So Manion began to put the pressure on by reminding him of what had happened in Zurich. I gather Manion was a great note passer during his trial?'

'None greater,' Geddy agreed.

'Well, one of his notes was on the back of that snapshot on which he had written something like "Adrian and Inge, Zurich, 27th August". It was, of course, enough to put the fear of God into Slatter. Perhaps, being a photograph, he didn't like to tear it up there and then. Possibly he felt someone was watching him at that moment. Anyway, he must have slipped it among his papers where it got caught up with something else and the next thing was it found its way here.'

Martin nodded slowly. 'I won't say it's always happening, but it's certainly not unknown. I remember once receiving a case to advise which was marked five guineas and the instructing solicitor had inadvertently enclosed a copy of his letter to the lay client in which he said that the moment had arrived to take Counsel's Opinion and this would cost ten guineas – those were the days when we were still paid in guineas. I may add that I never received any further work from those solicitors. But I'm interrupting you, Mr Roffey . . .'

'It seems that Slatter suddenly remembered the snapshot after Uppard had left with the papers, guessed what might have happened to it and hurried round here to find Appleman actually looking at it. One glance at Appleman's expression, moreover, was enough to tell him this was the end of the road so he killed him, removed the photo, retied the tape round the papers, after wiping them, to make it appear they'd not been opened, and made his escape.'

'You said earlier that there was an explanation for the uselessness of these further papers?' Geddy remarked.

'Yes. When Manion referred in his evidence to an important document his solicitor had which would prove his innocence, he was giving Slatter yet another chance to forge this letter I've mentioned. In the circumstances, Slatter had to produce something to you, so he sent round the documents you did receive.'

'I gather,' Martin said, 'that Slatter has made a pretty full confession?'

'He broke completely,' Roffey said in a tone full of satisfaction, 'once he realised that Manion had spilt all the beans. Incidentally, it was Manion, via Uppard, who sent me anonymously a copy of the snapshot. You might like to see it.' He brought it out of his pocket and tossed it, in its cellophane envelope, casually on to Martin's desk.

'It doesn't seem to me to matter how many copies he managed to destroy so long as Manion had the negative.'

Roffey nodded. 'There was a breaking – well, a technical breaking – at Manion's mews flat last Saturday night. Slatter's admitted to that, too. He'd had a key since Manion's arrest and went there looking for it.'

'Did he find it?'

'No.'

'Not there?'

Roffey gave a short laugh. 'The whereabouts of the negative is about the only thing Manion has refused to disclose so far. But I'm sure I'll be able to get it out of him if it becomes necessary.' He paused and looked at them with a complacent expression. 'And that, gentlemen, is about all.'

'Well, it remains for us only to congratulate you and to thank you. As you can well imagine, it's a considerable relief to all of us in Chambers that your enquiries have been brought to a conclusion. It's been a traumatic time for everyone but clearly as events turn out it might have been worse.'

Martin rose, but Roffey remained seated.

'What's happened to Mr Quant?' he enquired. 'I'm told he's gone abroad suddenly.'

'He's not been well for some time. Overwork, strain. The Bar can be a most demanding taskmaster, you know.'

'Even so, it seems to have hit him very suddenly.'

'There always has to be the straw which breaks the camel's back.'

'What was it in his case, I wonder?'

'I've no idea,' Martin said blandly, meeting Roffey's keen gaze head on. He walked across and picked up Roffey's bowler hat and umbrella. 'Well, Mr Roffey, my congratulations again. At least one thing's certain, neither the defence nor the prosecution briefs will be coming to these Chambers.'

XXV

Sheila spotted Alan as soon as she entered the bar. He was sitting over in a corner scanning the pages of an evening paper with a furious frown on his face. An almost untouched pint of beer sat on the table in front of him.

He glanced up only when Sheila stood over him. 'Hello, it says in the stop-press that Slatter's been charged, but I can't find anything else about it at all. There must be something on one of the pages.' His voice was tetchy. 'Have you heard anything more?'

'I'll have a gin and tonic please,' Sheila said firmly.

'Oh yes, sorry. Hang on and I'll get you one.' When he returned with her drink, he said, 'You must know something more than is in the paper.'

'Roffey left Chambers just before I did, but he wasn't talking to the lower orders. He spent about forty-five minutes with Mr Ainsworth and Mr Geddy, but I've no idea what he said to them.'

'But it is true that Slatter has been charged?'

'Yes.'

Alan let out a long sigh of relief. 'Thank God, it's all over, then!'

'Maybe it's not the only thing that's all over!'

He looked at her with a puzzled frown. 'What exactly do you mean?'

'I'm referring to you and me.'

'What the hell are you getting at?'

'I'm trying to say, Alan, that I'm not sure we're right for each other.'

'You're not serious, Sheil?'

'I've done a lot of thinking these past twenty-four hours and ... and ... well, I'm not sure. I want more time to sort out my thoughts.'

'But what have I done?' he asked, his face suddenly crumpled in dismay.

'It's the whole business of the murder, it's had an effect on us. It's idle to pretend otherwise. It's injected a sort of poison.'

He shook his head disbelievingly. 'But you backed me up, Sheil; you've been supporting me all along. You wouldn't have done that if you didn't love me.'

'Maybe I still love you, I just don't know. But it's because of what you've done and I've done that things can't ever be quite the same again.'

'All we did was protect one another.'

'You mean, I protected you! You lied to the police and ...'

'You did, too!'

'Yes, for your sake.'

'But it was natural to lie in the circumstances. Anyone would have.'

'I'm not sure.'

'After all, I didn't kill Appleman.'

'Perhaps not, but you were certainly in a mood to when you shot back to Chambers that night.'

'Well, he'd been pestering you, foisting his unwanted attentions on you. You said so, you were all upset when we met because of the way he'd been behaving.'

'I know.'

'Well then, all I intended was to have it out with him. It was a natural reaction. He had no right to try and get all amorous with you. I'd never have murdered him. I might have thumped him one, but that's all. Anyway, he was already dead when I got there.' He paused and shook his head disbelievingly. His tone was no more than a hoarse whisper when he went on, 'God, he was a terrible sight! I'll never get it out of my mind as long as I live. The blood ... the terrible expression on his face ... I was petrified. You know I was, Sheil.'

'I still wish we'd told the truth.'

'It's all very well saying that now someone's been arrested, but you never suggested it at the time.'

'I know.'

'They were only white lies we told.'

'I wish I could believe that.'

'You're not going to tell the police the truth now?' he asked in sudden alarm. 'It would still wreck us both.'

Pushing her half-finished gin and tonic away from her, she got up. 'I'm going, Alan. I won't do anything without letting you know and I'll get in touch with you quite soon, anyway.'

Speechless, Alan watched her leave.

*　　　*　　　*

183

Not far away, also sitting in a corner of a pub bar, David and Holly were having a drink. They had decided to avoid the Templar and the other pubs frequented by the Bar and had gone farther afield on this occasion.

David was drinking Guinness and Holly had a small lemon shandy.

'It's difficult to think of someone like Adrian Slatter as a murderer,' Holly said.

'Not all murderers are Christies or Haighs. In fact, most of them are ordinary people like you and me.'

'I can't imagine myself ever killing anyone deliberately.'

'Put like that nor can I see myself doing so. But I can conceive of circumstances arising in which I might suddenly lash out, so to speak. To the law, it would still be murder, even though it was unpremeditated in a lay sense. Anyway, Adrian Slatter's not the first solicitor to be charged with murder. There was a famous case years ago involving a solicitor who poisoned his wife and he was hanged.'

'Have any barristers ever been tried for murder?' Holly asked with interest.

'If they haven't, it's probably only because they're too artful to get caught.'

'It's like an exclusive club our profession, isn't it? I mean the way Martin and James are not letting on to anyone what's happened to Philip. They were quite ready to pass on to us everything Roffey had told them about the case, but they also made it very clear that Philip's abrupt disappearance from Chambers was not a subject for discussion.'

David nodded. 'Yes, senior ranks have certainly closed against everyone so far as the truth about Philip is concerned.

'I don't suppose we shall ever know what his row with Robin was about.'

'I don't suppose we shall,' David said without the flutter of an eyelid. If he had discovered the truth for himself he would probably have told Holly, but, as it was, it had come

184

to him in strictest confidence from Martin Ainsworth who had decided, as an afterthought, that he was entitled to be told primarily as Philip Quant's pupil but also as a co-pupil of Robin's.

David's immediate reaction had been one of utter shock, much more so than if Philip had been arrested for murder. Such is the power of convention, he later reflected wryly, that society is likely to react with less abhorrence if one man kills another than if he makes a pass at him. For this was what Philip Quant had done to Robin and it constituted, David agreed, a piece of dirty linen which no right-minded member of Chambers would want to see washed in public.

'A penny for your thoughts,' Holly said.

He looked at her and smiled. He was thinking that, despite its tendency to foster pomposity and, at times, an almost suffocating aura of corporate self-satisfaction, the Bar provided as agreeable working conditions as any young man could want. It was simply a question of side-stepping these pitfalls – as every young barrister before him had also realised. Happily, some had even managed to remember it in later life.

His smile broadened into a grin. 'Race you to our first brief,' he said.

>>> If you've enjoyed this book and would like to discover more great vintage crime and thriller titles, as well as the most exciting crime and thriller authors writing today, visit: >>>

The Murder Room
Where Criminal Minds Meet

themurderroom.com